THE DAY I KILLED JAMES

THE DAY I KILLED JAMES

CATHERINE RYAN HYDE

Alfred A. Knopf
New York

THIS IS A BORZOI BOOK PUBLISHED BY ALFRED A. KNOPF

Visit us on the Web! www.randomhouse.com/teens

Educators and librarians, for a variety of teaching tools, visit us at www.randomhouse.com/teachers

The Library of Congress has cataloged the hardcover edition of this work as follows:
Hyde, Catherine Ryan.
The day I killed James / Catherine Ryan Hyde.
p. cm.
Summary: Seventeen-year-old Theresa tries to get past the guilt she feels over the death of a neighbor who loved her, first through a journal her therapist tells her to keep, then by transforming herself and starting a new life.
ISBN 978-0-375-84158-3 (trade) — ISBN 978-0-375-94158-0 (lib. bdg.) —
ISBN 978-0-375-84960-2 (e-book)
[1. Guilt—Fiction. 2. Death—Fiction. 3. Love—Fiction. 4. Self-actualization (Psychology)—Fiction. 5. Psychotherapy—Fiction. 6. Diaries—Fiction. 7. California—Fiction.] I. Title.
PZ7.H96759Day 2008
[Fic]—dc22
2007049026

ISBN 978-0-440-23999-4 (tr. pbk.)

Printed in the United States of America
October 2010
10 9 8 7 6 5 4 3 2 1

First Trade Paperback Edition

PART ONE

Journal Entry _____

Day I'm writing this: Seventeen days
     after "The Day"
Day I'm writing about: Today

People die of love. I'm one of the few who'll admit it. That doesn't mean it isn't true.

Take all the people who died yesterday, or last week, or last year. Subtract all the suicides and the so-called accidents of the brokenhearted. Take away the men who got blown away for being in the wrong bed at the wrong moment, the women in abusive marriages who died of cancer because they couldn't find any other exit from their lives. All the AIDS deaths except from the needles and the transfusions, the ones they call the innocent victims. Like if you have sex, you're guilty. Deserved just what you got.

Now tell me who all you've got left.

Without love the world would be overpopulated, except that without love it wouldn't be populated at all.

3

Love giveth and love taketh away and all that crap. You'll probably say all those people died from the lack of love, but I say it's two sides of the same coin. So it's the same coin.

Today was my third session with Dr. Grey.

He said, "I was hoping by now you'd be letting your hair grow out."

I said, "I brought in another news clipping."

"God, Theresa, must we again? Okay. Fine. If you really still need to do this. Fine." Or something like that. He said some collection of words that added up to something like that.

I didn't read it to him. Not as such. Just sort of paraphrased. Just told him the gist of the article, how this woman in New York turned her back on her three-year-old daughter's stroller just long enough to buy a newspaper out of a rack. Turned back to find an empty stroller. Six days later they still have no idea. Maybe they never will.

I felt sorry for this woman, because what the woman did to her daughter was so much less premeditated than what I did to James. But I didn't say so.

Dr. Grey sat for a time in silence, as if mentally counting to ten. "I can't make all the progress on my own, you know."

"You're the professional," I said. "Do your job."

"I am," he said. "Do yours."

I'm not getting on all that well with Dr. Grey. I've thought of dumping him and getting somebody else, but that would be the easy way out, which I'm not entirely sure I deserve. And besides, my father is paying for this. And I'm not anxious to explain why it isn't working out.

Then I told him about the tattoo. Which is part of why I got it, to show to Dr. Grey. A nice, clean argument, one that wouldn't take too much out of me. So I showed it to him. Took off my big outer shirt and there it was.

Carefully planned. Blood-red, so everyone would know what kind of fluid I'm losing. Right over my heart, so they'd know from where. And also shaped like a heart, the tattoo. With a banner across that says JAMES. Because I know James would do as much for me.

Dr. Grey said, "I'm not going to pretend I don't consider this backsliding."

"*I* don't consider it backsliding," I said. And I was comfortable in that. I was, just at that moment, comfortable in everything but the six-day-old tattoo, which still itched and peeled like a mean sunburn.

"What do you consider it, Theresa?"

"A lifelong commitment."

"To someone who's dead."

"Absolutely. He hasn't abandoned his commitment to me just because he's dead."

Then I caught myself on patchy ice, because I wisely had not told Dr. Grey about some of James's tender manifestations of late, like the songs he plays for me on my car radio. I've barred myself from speaking of that in therapy, just as Dr. Grey barred me from referring to that day as "The Day I Killed James." He says I came here to learn not to say that, so start practicing. Now I have one hour a week, one spot on the planet, where I don't say that. I call it "The Day." It's just an abbreviation, but it seems to make Dr. Grey happy.

"How do you assess a dead man's commitment?"

"Call it a gut feeling." Then I said—and, mind you, it was probably a big mistake, but that's me—I said, "The day after I killed James I woke up alive. And that's a thing for which I can never quite forgive myself."

He gave me a slightly tentative look. Maybe he didn't get what I meant. The part about waking up alive. The part about not forgiving myself is self-explanatory. Maybe he understood perfectly but was deciding whether to call me on saying "the day after I killed James." I thought I was allowed to say that. I thought only the day itself was off-limits.

I didn't go on. But *I* knew what I meant. About waking up alive.

The day after I killed James, I woke up, and stood up, and took stock of myself. I had all my arms, and my legs, and my toes, and everything seemed to work, only not quite as readily as before. Not with the same lack of forethought.

I just woke up, and I was someone I'd never tried on before.

And I'll tell you who I was. I was that person who walks away from a deadly rail disaster. Everybody mostly killed on impact, but then there's always that one person just wandering loose and nobody can figure out how. Just walking around looking lost.

This person will appear unharmed to you. Do not be fooled.

Journal Entry

Day I'm writing this: Eighteen days
    after "The Day"
Day I'm writing about: Today

Today a guy tried to pick me up in a bookstore. Are you ready for that? I was actually saying that out loud, in fact, later, on the way home: "Are you ready for that?" I shave my head, I've lost almost twenty pounds. I wear truckloads of loose clothing. I mean, what do I have to do?

"Buy you a cappuccino?" he asked when he'd caught my attention.

I looked at him like a kestrel might. We're small, kestrels and me, but we can be formidable.

"Do you love life?" I asked.

He smiled. Looked confused for a moment. I suppose he thought it was part of a dating questionnaire. Like, Do you enjoy sharing hot chocolate and long walks on the beach at sunset?

"I do," he said. "I love life."

"Then run."

He didn't, exactly. But he did go away.

Journal Entry

```
Day I'm writing this: Nineteen days
    after "The Day"
Day I'm writing about: Four days
    after "The Day"
```

Not long after I killed James, I did something that's always been hard for me to do. I asked for help.

It's not that I'm proud. I'm not that proud. I'm not sure why it's so hard for me. Maybe because there's really no one there to ask. My mother is long gone. And my poor father so badly wants me not to need any help. I guess because he doesn't have any. I guess it would be like asking for a billion dollars. He's hoping I won't. So he won't have to say, Sorry, but I can't give you what I don't have myself.

Then there are my friends, of which I recently had many. Frieda is my best bud, of course, but there's also Christie and Johnna and Paulette and Ann. And Harry and Bobby and Heather. And Shanni. Why I couldn't ask them, I'm not entirely sure. Maybe I just see them as busy with their own lives. Or maybe I didn't get enough practice at home.

Anyway, I was desperate. So I asked my dad. I said, "I can't do this alone. I have no idea how. It's more than I can hold up, and I have no idea which way to go. I need help."

I noticed he was refusing to meet my eyes. Not a real good sign.

He's a nice guy, my father. He just needs a little help himself.

Then, sensing that I wasn't doing very well, I added a desperate cherry to my cry-for-help sundae. "Please."

To make a long story short, he bought me Dr. Grey.

Hopefully that clarifies why I don't get along so well with Dr. Grey.

I mean, does it? Or am I being weird?

Thing is, when you ask someone for help, it means you want them to help you. It does not mean you hope they'll purchase help from a total stranger and throw it in your direction, closing the issue.

I cried all night.

Then, the first time I went to see Dr. Grey, I told him I was angry about it.

He said it sounded like I was hurt.

I said, "No. I'm angry."

He said, "Anger tends to cover hurt."

I said, "Tendencies are not absolute."

He said, "This one pretty much is, though."

I said, "Now I'm even angrier."

It's hard to explain why I wouldn't own it. After all, angry people don't tend to cry all night. But it has something to do with a decision I made. That night. While I was crying.

I decided I was in a painful no-man's-land of emotion and I had to go one way or the other. I either had to pour myself at the feet of my family and friends like a puddle of badly set Jell-O, or I had to put on a suit of armor and face the rest of my life as an army of one.

I guess it's pretty obvious what I decided. But I'm not even sure "decided" is the right word. Because one of those options would have been absolutely impossible for me.

It's like deciding whether to jump off a cliff or fly. Assuming you're not a bird, that is. Decide what you want, but really it comes down to one possible option. And once you jump off the cliff, getting back up on it is more or less out of the question, too.

I keep thinking of those cheesy movies and dime-store novels that start with lines like, "I wasn't always like this. Once I was young and happy like you."

But why dwell on ancient history?

ONE

I'm Sorry I Washed Your Car

Maybe I should have been nicer about it. But it was early. It was so damned early. It was daybreak, damn it to hell. And I didn't have to get up for school yet. And that's one of those things it just doesn't pay to rush.

I guess I should have been nicer about a lot of things. But that's hindsight. Isn't it?

I couldn't just roll over and go back to sleep, because there was water running somewhere. And there shouldn't have been.

So I rolled out of bed and put on Randy's red pin-striped shirt. I love that shirt. If we—God forbid—ever break up, he'd better kiss it goodbye. And I went to the window. And there was James in the driveway, washing my car.

I opened the window. Thought that would get his

attention, but not quite. Usually it was not hard for me. To get James's attention.

I waved my arms around. Without raising them too high, because, you know, Randy's shirt only covered just so much. And James was easily encouraged. Pre-encouraged, one might even say. Like one of those computers you buy with the software already installed.

He saw me then. Snapped off the hose. Smiled. When James smiled at me, it made me a little bit nervous. When he smiled at me, his face lit up with this look that always made me wonder why being loved is not the joy the poets claim.

James or Randy, either one. It's just not what they set us up to expect.

He called out good morning to me.

"James," I said, trying to be half-assed quiet to keep my father out of it. My father was not so sure about the whole James phenomenon. "Why are you washing my car?"

It's really pathetic, what happened to that poor smile. It reminded me of a dog told to play dead. James had this way of making me feel bad. Life has this way of making me feel bad.

"Don't you want me to?" he asked. "I'm sorry."

How do I answer a question like that?

So I just looked up at the sky, which seemed somewhat black and expectant, and I said, "I think maybe it's going to rain."

"If it does," James said, "it will be all my fault. Because I washed your car. Do you want me to stop now? I'd at least have to rinse off this soap."

I didn't know if I wanted James to wash my car. I'd never really thought about it. It was too early to think about it when I was put on the spot to say. But one thing I did know for sure.

I said, "I definitely do not want you to wash my car and then apologize for it."

"Right," he said. "Sorry. I mean . . . you know what I mean."

I closed the window. My father stuck his head in through my door. The hose sound kicked in again from the driveway.

"Who are you talking to?" my father asked. "Why are you making so much noise? You woke me up. Why did you wake me?"

"You have to get up now anyway," I said, looking at the clock. "You'll be late for work."

He reached for my alarm clock. Knocked it over onto its back. "Aw, crap. Why didn't you wake me?"

I said, "I did wake you, remember? That's what you were just complaining about."

See, it even extends to parents. What I said about love.

It rained. I can't entirely claim it's because James washed my car, because it rained days later. But it felt satisfying, somehow, to blame this and that on James.

I was sitting at the dining room table paying bills. Because somebody had to do it.

When I looked out the window it was raining in sheets, and I swore I saw James skate by. Along the driveway toward the garage. It was like a moment of action in bad animation. You know how when they're really hard up for animation dollars they move a static character across a static scene? Like that.

His hair was still short from that two-year stint in the Air Force. So the fact of being soaking wet didn't change his look much. He had a hat, but he wasn't wearing it. Just holding it by the brim. And then that was it. He just slid out of my field of view.

A moment later he came by in the other direction. Garage to street. Without his shirt. Hat in hand. Wearing a strappy sleeveless undershirt like the kind my uncle Gerry used to wear. Only, I have to say it, it looked better on James.

He'd certainly buffed up while he was away.

I couldn't decide if this was a fun game or not. Probably not.

On the third trip by, no noticeable change. Which made me wonder suddenly if he was still wearing his pants. Which made me jump up to see. Which made James laugh and point, like, I got you. I made you look.

He was wearing his pants. But he made me look.

What he was not wearing were skates. He was just sliding. Hydroplaning along the fresh concrete of my driveway in a quarter-inch sheet of standing water. Which didn't seem a good enough explanation until I realized he was sliding down the trail of automatic transmission fluid my crappy old hand-me-down car deposits on its way to and from the garage.

James was always telling me to get that fixed. He'd even offered to replace my pan gasket, an offer I'd several times refused. If I had been foolish enough to let him in just then, he likely would've offered again.

Once he had my attention, something happened to his. He failed to cut off the skid in time. He sort of bounced off our garage door. Then he recovered his poise and began to dance. It reminded me of a cat after it loses face. That sort of "I meant to do that" attitude. He looked pretty smooth, actually. Dancing. It was this old-fashioned Gene Kelly sort of a thing. Not half bad.

Then all of a sudden there was my father. Right at my left shoulder.

He said, "What in God's name is he doing?"

I said, "Apparently a scene from *Singin' in the Rain*."

He said, "The guy has no shame."

I said, "How can you say that, Dad? He's adorable. He's just being playful."

"You just described a golden retriever puppy. He has no shame because he doesn't even bother to pretend he's not in love with you when I'm around."

"Yes, he does. He can't see you from there."

"Of course he can."

"No, he can't. Come over here."

So he moved over to where James could see him. James slipped on a patch of transmission fluid. His feet came right out from underneath him. He landed on his hip and one elbow, and just lay there. Looking vaguely disoriented.

My father said, "Ouch."

I said, "I told you he didn't know you were here."

He said, "You really ought to get that transmission looked at."

Journal Entry _____

Day I'm writing this: Twenty days
    after "The Day"
Day I'm writing about: One day after
    "The Day"

The morning after I killed James I was sitting in the back of that highway patrol car, with the door open. And the guy had his boot up on the backseat, writing on a clipboard on his knee. Writing out a report.

I thought he was going to take me in, but he never did.

I read the report upside down. It listed me as the person who reported him missing. In the space marked RELATIONSHIP it said "Friend." It said I was James's friend.

Which I suppose was a euphemistic way of saying we were hooked up with each other, that kind of modern lumping together of a guy and a girl. It manifests into all kinds of sick, impermanent shapes, this new category.

But, *was* I James's friend?

I bet he thought so. I bet he trusted me to be at least that much.

Journal Entry

Day I'm writing this: Twenty-one
   days after "The Day"
Day I'm writing about: Yesterday

Yesterday evening I hitchhiked up the coast. I've been hitchhiking a lot lately. I've been tempting fate, to see if it wants to hurt me. Like walking down a dark street in a bad neighborhood with a bulging purse and a Rolex. Like, Here I am. Hurt me.

Nothing went wrong.

I got off about a mile south of the scene, even though the guy I rode up with could have driven me right to it.

You can't miss the spot now, because I put up a road-side cross with a wreath. Rainy season may take its toll, but it won't be rainy season again for nearly a year. I slept on a little patch of cold dirt on the hill side of the road. Had the dream again.

Roaring at that cliff, doing about sixty, with the

engine noise in my ears, and then I shoot off over the edge and everything goes silent. The bike falls away. Just hanging there in the sky in the dark. Even though I don't suppose the engine would stall, really, just because the ground fell away. I figure he heard it all the way down. Fell with it. But in the dream, all went silent in the dark, and I did not immediately fall. Like a cartoon character who has to notice first. Notice that the ground is gone before gravity becomes the law.

The fall was sudden, and I jolted awake.

I rediscovered myself by the side of the cold road, within walking distance of nothing.

I'm never sure if the person in the dream is James or me.

The moon was a crescent setting over the water, yellowish and indistinct. I wanted James to be somewhere near, but I couldn't feel him. But, see, I was still wanting him to do for me. That's how selfish I know I am.

A car came around the curve. Stopped, cut its lights, and two guys got out. I felt it in my stomach. I had asked for this. Too late to unask for it now. They weren't much older than me, maybe twenty. They stood over me.

"You okay?"

"Sure."

"Don't see a car. You got a car?"

"Not close."

"Need a ride?"

"No. I'm okay here."

They looked at each other in the dark. Good

Samaritans. The Universe just will not do it to me. They sat down, one on either side.

"You sure you're okay?"

I started to cry. That's embarrassing. I hate that. I don't even like to cry when I'm alone. That's a bad deal all the way around. Where was my suit of armor when I really needed it? Plus, so far as I could tell, I still couldn't fly.

One of them put an arm around my shoulder.

I told them everything. I confessed.

They drove me to San Simeon, where I could make a phone call. Figure my way home. I had money and my father's credit card, which no one had the good grace to steal from me.

Just as I was waving goodbye to them, the driver leaned out the window. He said, "You know, I've had girls do me worse than that."

I assume he was trying to be helpful.

But it's like saying, People fire guns at other people all the time. And lots of their intended targets are still alive.

Still, if you hit someone, you're responsible.

Maybe I'm too good an aim.

TWO

Shark Bait

Randy was planning something. How did I know? Because I knew him. Because after seven months, you can see things coming. And I knew it was going to be soon, because things were way too good between us. That always made him nervous.

And also, he'd been extra sweet lately, which is a bad sign.

I figured probably he'd tell me he was thinking of trying for a college out of town. Case Western in Cleveland or some shit like that. Or he'd say he needed more space, not quite so trite on the wording but that's what it'd add up to. Or maybe he'd say we should take a vacation from this thing. Or, God forbid, start seeing other people.

He does this now and then. All hell breaks loose. I spend a few weeks crying and asking him to reconsider, and that convinces him that I still care. When things are too quiet between us he forgets that I care.

So he backs off. He isn't really going to college in Cleveland. He only thought he needed a vacation until he realized how much he needed *me*.

Then things are good for a while, like they are now. Which is a really bad sign.

Yes, of course there's part of me that wants to get off this ride.

Along which lines I made a decision. I was not going to play the game this time. I even talked it over with Frieda. Who said, "Oh, whoa. This should be totally interesting. Tell me every detail. Whoa. Big stuff."

Maybe she didn't think I had it in me.

This time I was going to say, Okay, Randy. Fine. I will e-mail you every day in Cleveland. And as far as seeing other people, James will be happy to hear we've made that decision. James. You do so know who he is. My cute, older next-door neighbor. You know, the one who's so crazy about me? I can't wait to tell him the good news.

How Randy would handle all of this, I honestly didn't know. But this whole pattern of his, it was beginning to smack of a bluff. And what is a bluff for, if not to be called?

And besides, now Frieda was so hot on the idea I couldn't very well back out.

So anyway, on the morning in question I was still asleep. I was having this dream about a shark. I was just minding my own business, floating around in the ocean on my surfboard.

Actually, I don't have a surfboard. Actually, I've never surfed in my life, but dreams are like that.

I was sitting up on this thing, straddling it, my legs hanging into the water. Feeling the slight roll of the ocean. All very serene.

Then I looked down and saw it roaring at me at hundreds of miles per hour. About the size of a bus. I could only see a shadow of it, a gray outline, which actually made it worse. Ducking was out of the question. No time. Also no place to go. If he wants you, he's got you.

Then something propelled me out of sleep. Almost from there to the ceiling.

Well, probably at no time did my body leave the bed, but that was how it felt.

I sat up a second, trying to breathe. Full flight response, my heart pounding. And then it happened again, and I realized it was the phone.

It was only about seven a.m.

It was Randy.

He said, "You know that party at Frieda's? Don't get weirded out. But I thought I might go with Rachel Lindstrom. I mean, I know you figured we'd go, but it was just sort of an assumption, right? I mean, we didn't talk it out or anything. And we always do, so this'll just be sort of . . . different. You know?"

Long silence on the line. I just sat there on my surfboard like a sitting-duck fool. Here's what he said next. This is the shark attack in a nutshell.

"We never really talked about seeing other people. So

I figured it wasn't . . . like . . . if we didn't say we couldn't, then . . ."

Well, not a concise nutshell. But that's the short version.

There was something I was going to do about all this. When it happened. What was that great plan again?

"Um . . . can I call you right back?"

Another very weird silence, and then I gently set the phone back in its cradle. Why gently, I don't know. I just remember thinking how bizarre it was, that even in my sleep I had seen that one coming.

I called Frieda right away. Knowing her, she might even have been up. I just hoped I didn't get one of her parents. They were both heavy drinkers. Maybe they'd be in a bad mood if I woke them. Then again, maybe waking them was an impossibility.

Three rings.

"Oh, pick up your damn phone, Frieda!"

She obeyed immediately.

Frieda's voice, like a glass of cool water. "Hi, sweetie. How are you?"

"He says he's coming to your party with Rachel Lindstrom."

"Whoa. How long has this been going on?"

"He didn't say it was going on. He didn't say anything was going on. It was more like . . . a potential something. Like something . . . maybe could. Go on. He didn't say it was. Already."

It was dawning on me—the more I denied this—that I was in denial about this.

"And you said so be it and thanked him for his honesty. Right?"

"Not exactly."

"Oh God. What did you say?"

"I said, 'I'll call you back.' And then I called *you*."

"Call him back and tell him to do whatever he needs to do."

"But then he will."

"And if you tell him not to, he will anyway."

"God, I hate you, Frieda."

"I love you, too, sweetie. Good luck."

He picked up on the first ring.

"Okay, Randy. Thanks for your honesty. What do we do now?"

"Um . . ." I could tell that was not the onslaught he had been prepared to counter. "I guess we try being apart for a while."

I could hear in his voice that this was hard for him, which made it hard for me. If he had done these things toyingly, like a house cat that's caught itself something helpless, that would be one thing. But this obviously came from such a depth of sincere pathology that I felt sorry for him, and for a moment I almost forgot to feel sorry for myself. Almost.

"So we'll both just be seeing someone else."

"Excuse me?" His voice changed. As if someone had slapped him for a transgression not yet identified. "You met someone, too?"

"Well, you know. James."

"James?" he said. Loudly. I had struck a nerve. Good. "James? How could you be interested in James? He's about *twenty*."

"Twenty-two."

"He's older. He's like . . . twenty-two? He isn't even your age. He's like . . ."

"Here's a lesson for you, Randy, since you've obviously been out of touch with the dating scene too long. An older guy is not the liability you make it out to be."

He sulked for a moment in silence.

"Are you sure this is what you want?" he said.

I laughed out loud. Probably just a release of tension. "You forgot who started this."

He hung up the phone.

Frieda would be proud of me. On the outside, that had looked pretty good. On the inside, life as I had known it was at least seriously wounded. Bleeding *and* on fire. If not DOA.

Okay. There's a lot to know about Frieda's place, her parents. Her living situation. It's a lot to fill in as I go, but here's trying.

Frieda lives at the end of my street, but the end of my street is nearly a mile down. The houses on my street are just that. Houses. Not ranches or farms or acreage. But when you get to the end of the street, there's Frieda's place. And it's a ranch. We live close to the edge of town.

It used to be a working horse ranch. Frieda's father used to be a successful horse trainer. Now he's only successful at drunkenness. Good thing the place is all paid for.

There are no longer any horses on this ranch. But there's a barn. A very big, empty barn. With a little room upstairs that I guess was designed to house a stable hand. And about twenty stalls that always seem lonely to me. I think stalls get lonely without horses.

This barn is where we intend on having our party. And the theme of the party is ever so simple. No more high school. Ever. We are graduating and getting out and that's good.

This barn is also where I got drunk on tequila shooters following Randy's shark call.

We were not in the barn to hide our drinking from her parents. This time of the evening you wouldn't need to hide a herd of elephants from her parents. They go into their own little country early on. It's sad.

So we were up on the bed in that little upstairs barn room. Frieda's dog, Leevon, was lying in between us, on his back, with all four feet sticking up. He's a cool dog, Leevon. Kind of like a border collie, only not really. All white except for a patch of black on one eye. He's my bud.

I said, "Why are we not in the house again?"

She said, "Because there's no phone out here."

"Oh. Okay." So far there was no alcohol in play. "Why is that a good thing again?"

"Because I don't want you to call Randy."

"I'm not going to call Randy."

"I'm not so sure."

"Why would I do that?"

"I don't know. Why did you do that every time before?"

This is when I felt myself suddenly overcome with depression. The whole world felt very hopeless. This is also when I said the following regrettable thing. "I want to get drunk."

She looked at me like I was from Mars. Normally I knew I was not. On that particular evening it was not outside the realm of possibility.

"You don't drink."

"I could make an exception."

"You hate people who drink. You think drinking is stupid."

"I think I might have been waiting for just such an occasion." A pause. "I might not be able to come to your party."

"You can't miss the party. It's going to be the biggest thing ever. Don't let Randy make you miss that."

"I don't think I can handle it."

"Invite James. That'll teach him."

"I don't want to do that to James. It would be using him."

"From what little I know of James, he might see that as a good thing."

"I need more time to think about this." What I needed was everything back to normal. And/or a stiff drink. "I was serious with what I said about the drunk thing."

She shrugged. Then she went off in the direction of the house to see what her parents had lying around. In retrospect I can tell you it was tequila. At the time it could have been anything. And everything.

The minute she left, I slipped my cell phone out of my pocket. Called Randy.

"Randy, listen," I said. "I can't keep doing this. This is too hard. This just hurts too much every time. If you want to be with me, be with me. Call her right now and tell her it's over." But that was a shock to my careful system of denial. I didn't want it to be over, I wanted it to never have begun. "I mean, tell her it's not going to start. That there'll never be anything. If you do that, come over after. Come over tonight so I can look into your eyes and see you really did it. If you don't come over, then I don't want to see you or talk to you again."

"Theresa, I—"

"I mean it, Randy. I can't keep doing this. I'm sorry."

"Do I get to say anything?"

"Only after I hang up."

And I did.

I looked over at Leevon. He was doing that thing he sometimes does, where he puts one paw over his muzzle like he's trying to cover his eyes. But I have no doubt that this was purely coincidental.

Or not much doubt, anyway.

```
Day I'm writing this: Twenty-two
    days after "The Day"
Day I'm writing about: Today
```

I found another clipping. A teenage girl in Utah. Had her driver's license for three weeks, and she was driving down the highway, changing the radio station. Before she could look up again, she drifted over and killed a cyclist riding on the shoulder.

It's still not quite what I'm looking for.

I mean, nobody would say, You son of a bitch, how could you do something so callous as to change a radio station?

I'm still looking for somebody who was guilty of something really bad when it happened. Somewhere in the world, just one person as awful as me.

We could form a support group.

They have those "Women Who Love Too Much"

groups. We could form a "Women Who Blame Themselves" group. We could help each other blame ourselves.

Dr. Grey is no good for that at all.

Speaking of Dr. Grey, today was my fifth session.

I asked him a question.

I said, "Did love become very dangerous that day? Or did it always have that potential and I just didn't notice?"

It seems to please him, that I ask questions now. It's almost like talking. Almost like therapy.

"It always had the potential."

"Then why do we all use it so lightly?"

"We drive cars lightly, and cars kill people all the time."

"Not that teenage girl in Utah. She doesn't drive lightly. I bet she doesn't drive now at all."

"Maybe she drives carefully. Maybe she'll drive carefully for years, and nobody will get hurt. And after a while she may relax a little bit."

"Not completely, though."

"No," he admitted. "Not completely."

It seemed potentially significant to me that Dr. Grey and I agreed about something.

Journal Entry

Day I'm writing this: Twenty-three
    days after "The Day"
Day I'm writing about: "The Day"

Right after I killed James—before I knew I had yet—I spent a lot of the day thinking what I'd say to him when he got home.

Maybe he wouldn't have been speaking to me. He might have been furious with me, or just depressed with himself in general.

I would have applied for his forgiveness in triplicate. It might have taken a couple of years to come through. But, eventually, we might have been friends again. Or for the first time, I'm not sure. But then the Highway Patrol showed up and I slowly realized that he'd just frozen all that.

Now we're locked in that moment forever, like

breaking a clock at one-fifteen, and no matter how much time goes by it's always one-fifteen according to that clock. That whole process of understanding has been taken out of my reach.

How is that fair?

THREE

Bringing Your New Puppy Home

A young man in love has no soul. Of his own, I mean. No substance. I'm not saying a young woman is any different, but how about if we take things one at a time?

Suddenly I had all this motivation to fall in love with James. Even a tidy case of lust would have done nicely. Because Randy had someone he felt that way about. It didn't seem fair.

But I didn't even remember James's last name. And more to the point, I had no idea at all who he was. Every time he came near me he left whoever the hell he was behind in order to be whatever the hell I wanted. And all I wanted was to know who the hell he was.

So far this was not working out at all.

Even when he was in the Air Force and wrote me all those letters. I learned everything about the Air Force and nothing about him.

When I got home from drinking tequila shooters with Frieda, I missed my own door and ended up at James's. It was an accident. I wonder why I just bothered to say it was an accident. I wonder if that means I'm not sure. Maybe it was one of those Freudian things. Or maybe it was one tequila shooter too many, and I'm investing too much significance in a simple drunken mistake.

I was fumbling around with my keys, and he came to the door.

I said, "James. What are you doing in my house?" I feel bad about the fact that I never just say, Hello, James. Ever. It's always a question, usually about why he's doing what he's doing. I would have to do better with that. Sometime. When I was sober.

He said, "Theresa. Wow. We better get you home."

And I guess we got me home, because that's where I woke up. But to back up again for a minute . . .

When we got me to my door, I was trying too hard. I wanted it to be true, what I told Randy about him. I wanted James to be my special exciting somebody new. Otherwise Randy had one of those and I had nothing. So I guess I was pushing at it.

I threw myself at him, literally. But I doubt he knew that's what it was. Fell into his arms and held him and felt his warmth and said to myself, There. I feel it. It's right there. Really. I'm not making it up.

I was making it up. It was just like hugging my brother. I mean, if I'd had a brother.

I kissed his cheek and said, "You're sweet, James. Really. I appreciate you."

Meanwhile I was thinking, If I open the door and Randy's not there, I'll die. If he doesn't come over tonight, if I know he's with her, I'll drop dead on the spot.

James waited while I opened the door.

Randy wasn't there.

James said several more things to me, and I might have even said a few things back, but I'm not sure. I don't remember. I was busy dying.

When I woke up the next morning, James was in the driveway, under my car. He had it up on jack stands, and all I could see was a mess of tools and his legs. But it had to be James. Who else would spontaneously perform an automotive repair for me?

I pulled on jeans and a sweater and took my coffee out to the driveway. I could have avoided all this by pulling my car into the garage last night. But it was a rough night, and the idea of getting out and opening the garage door had been too much for me. Actually, just making it home had been a stroke of luck. Good thing Frieda lived close.

James had offered to install an automatic garage door opener. Many times. I had yet to break down on that one.

I kicked his Nike lightly.

He said, "Good morning." Without bothering to slide out.

I said, "James, I know I ask this a lot. But what are you doing?"

He said, "Putting a new pan gasket on your transmission. You said I could. Remember?"

"I said that?"

"Last night. You really don't remember?"

"I was having a bad night."

Amen to that.

He knew. He seemed to remember.

He said, "I had to help you find your front door. I asked again about fixing your car. You said no. I said what harm could it do? You said it pisses Randy off. Then you said, 'Oh yeah. That's right. I don't have to worry about that anymore.'"

I should have worn my sunglasses. Out there in the bright old world. The inside of my head was not an attractive landscape, and shedding light on the subject hardly helped.

James grabbed the bumper and slid out from under my car, wiping his hands on a shop rag. Where did he get a shop rag? Not at my house. He must've brought one from home.

He said, "Did you break up with him?"

It's possible that he was trying not to sound hopeful. But if so it wasn't working. I didn't really want to talk about it. But it seemed easier to talk about it than talk my way out of it.

I said something fairly noncommittal.

I said, "Hard to say. Call it the first draft of a breakup. Never know what'll happen in the revisions."

I was still not a hundred percent convinced that all of it was real. Any of it, for that matter.

I was ready to stop talking. I was ready to go inside. I was ready to die.

Hadn't I meant to do that last night? When will I ever get that right?

James said, "Your car will be ready to go in an hour or two."

I said, "Then it's hours ahead of me."

And I went back to bed.

Sometime later I heard his motorcycle fire up and fade away down the block. Which I took to mean my car must be ready. Which made one of us. Damned if there was any place I wanted to be.

Actually, I figured he'd gone to work. Actually, it was Saturday, but at the moment I was not in clear focus about that. Actually, if it had been a working day for James it would have been a school day for me. Clearly I was not in clear focus about a lot of things.

A few hours later he came home. He'd had the gas tank on his motorcycle repainted. It was now stark white, with a red heart top center, with a blue banner across it, on which was painted my name.

Journal Entry

Day I'm writing this: Twenty-four
   days after "The Day"
Day I'm writing about: Before "The
   Day"

Turns out there were other things I'm not good at. Probably had been all along. Could I really have been that blind to myself all those years? Or did circumstances conspire to help me recognize my own well-hidden shortcomings?

I hate it when that happens.

Either way.

I went to school as usual after the shark attack. Only not as usual. Because I wasn't Randy's girlfriend anymore. As best I could figure, I wasn't.

Now, I'd been other guys' girlfriend. And before being, and in between being, I knew who I was. All by myself and not contingent on my status in their lives. And even while I was other guys' girlfriend, I was pretty much Theresa and that was okay. If memory serves.

But it was different somehow with Randy. Like I thought there would always be me and Randy, so now I had to start all my thinking over again. Like now I could be wrong about anything. Everything. But I'm getting off track. That wasn't my big discovery.

I discovered I'm very bad at letting people see me hurting.

Everyone knew about Rachel Lindstrom. Everyone. Paris Hilton could do something stupid and get less press. My brutal and senseless murder might have made fewer waves.

I guess we'd been sort of an "it" couple. Which I'm not entirely sure I knew. Or noticed. Maybe I'd have known it if I'd stopped to think about it, but I never had. I'd had no reason to look at us from the outside. Who does that, anyway?

Reaction was mixed.

A couple of the unpopular girls, who never seemed to notice that I smiled at them every chance I got, smirked.

My friends were very supportive. Every single one of them. One by one, as the day painfully progressed, they ran to my aid and said one thing or another that was exactly what I did not want or need to hear.

Shanni said, "He's a jerk." I still didn't really think he was. Or didn't want to, anyway.

The Guyfriends, Harry and Bobby, approached me in the cafeteria like a two-man comedy team. Intertwined in their condolences. Said, "We always thought you were too good for him." They seemed to mean it sincerely. I wanted to ask, Too good how? Why? In what way was I so good? I needed to hear that. But I didn't ask.

Heather said, "Oh. I heard about Randy and Rachel." In the voice one would use to say, Oh. I heard about your whole family being killed in that car crash. "You poor thing." I wanted to tell her she was ruining my careful system of denial regarding R. and R. But saying so would have ruined it just as surely.

Ann pulled me aside in gym class and asked gravely, "Are you okay?" I was tempted to say, I might be, if everyone could just stop asking me if I am. But no point lashing out at those who are trying to help you. However ineffectively.

Johnna said, "You give 'em everything and they cut your heart out. Every time." She was going through her own breakup, so at least I could console myself in knowing that she was really offering bad condolences to herself. Not me.

Christie just looked over her shoulder and smiled at me sadly in history. That, oddly enough, was the one that cut through the fog. Made me realize how bad I am at hurting in public.

Paulette was out sick that week, so I'll never know how she would have tormented me if she'd been healthier and more present.

To each one of them, I said almost exactly the same thing: "No worries. None at all. Just wait till you see the twenty-two-year-old buff hunk I'm planning to bring to Frieda's party. You'll die."

Seriously. It was pathetic.

It was also my one-way ticket into something I knew better than to do.

Journal Entry _____

Day I'm writing this: Twenty-five days
    after "The Day"
Day I'm writing about: Before "The
    Day"

Letting go is not a specialty of mine. In fact, it seems to be something I was born with. Or born without, I should say. Just a run-of-the-mill birth defect.

My mother used to like to tell a story. Before she ran off to Europe to rediscover herself without us. Or whatever the hell she did. It's hard to judge by my father's version of events. And, also, she may still like to tell this story. For all I know. Wherever she is. But I wouldn't hear it anymore, even if she did. Because of that whole Atlantic Ocean thing.

I think she doesn't think or talk about us at all now. But maybe I'm just being bitter. People say I'm bitter about her. I try not to be. But it's tricky.

Anyway, she used to tell this story of taking me to see *Alice in Wonderland*. On the way home in the car I was all twisted because they never did say why a raven is like a writing desk. I was still twisted the next day. And the following week.

When I was about thirteen it came up again, more or less out of nowhere. I still wanted to know why a raven is like a writing desk. I mean, how can you open a can of worms like that one and then just walk away?

My mother said, "Let it go, Theresa. Let it go."

Most advice comes without instructions.

Two days after I broke up with Randy, James took me for a ride on his motorcycle.

On the way up the coast together, I remembered that I didn't even remember James's last name. I mean, I must have known it at one time, because I wrote to him while he was in the Air Force. Not often, but I did. But in that moment it was gone from my head.

But we were riding up on his bike, the roar of the engine all around us and the wind whipping past our helmets, and it just didn't seem like the time to ask.

He stuck his arm straight out on the cliff side. Pointing at something. I realized too late it was a pointing thing. Never saw what he saw.

We got off and took a break in Ragged Point. Got two cups of coffee and leaned on the bike and drank them.

I said, "I know how terrible this is going to sound, and I'm really sorry. Really I am. But I have this total mental block on your last name. I know it. It's not that I don't know it. It's just one of those mental blocks. You know them, right? You know how they are."

I may have gone on even longer than that.

I got the sense he was just waiting patiently for me to shut up so he could talk.

He was a patient guy, James. Another thing we didn't have in common.

He said, "Stewart."

I said, "James Stewart?" Because, really. James Stewart? How could I have forgotten that?

He said, "Please don't make any of the obvious jokes. I've heard them all."

I said, "Deal." Then before I tossed my empty cup, I said, "What were you pointing at back there?"

He said, "A whale. Breaching."

I said, "There was a whale out there?"

He said, "There was."

I'd been so busy stressing about Randy and his new girlfriend, I'd forgotten to notice there was even an ocean out there. And, at least on this particular occasion, that is how I missed the whale.

Day I'm writing this: Twenty-six
    days after "The Day"
Day I'm writing about: The morning
    after "The Day"

The morning after I killed him, all the way up the coast I tried to explain that I didn't know enough about James. To the Highway Patrol guys, I mean.

I said, "He was my neighbor. But I don't even know if he had family or who they might be."

I said, "He lived next door to me for four years, but I didn't pay enough attention. He was kind of older. I was just a little girl. I mean, not a little girl, but . . . too little for *him*. I mean, most of that time. I was. Too young for him. I'm not even eighteen for three more days. And he was twenty-two."

I said, "It was a first date sort of a thing."

But when he left the party and never ended up anywhere, I'd been the one to phone it in. So now I owned him. Somebody had to own a missing person. All of a sudden we belonged to each other.

I said, "How much farther do we have to drive?"

In a weird regression to childhood, I thought, Are we there yet?

The guy said, "It's near Ragged Point."

By the time we arrived at the scene, a crane had been brought down from Caltrans in Gorda. They were pulling James's bike back up from the rocks below, onto the road. More or less in one piece, but not looking much like a motorcycle.

They set it down in the dirt on the cliff side of the road. All the officers looked at me. Stared at me and waited.

"Yes," I said. "That is my friend James Stewart's motorcycle." As I was talking, I was marveling at the fact that I was talking. How was I doing that? Was I really doing that? I couldn't feel it. It sounded like me, but I didn't really feel that. Or anything else, really. Then I heard myself say, "Am I done here now? I mean, can I go?"

I know that sounded callous. I didn't mean it to. I swear.

It was actually a terrified moment of self-defense. What I meant was, Am I in custody? Or am I free? And that's a very important question. Even at a time like that.

A sheriff's deputy was studying the tire tracks. He said there had been no braking and no skid.

"Meaning what, exactly?" I said, though he clearly had not been talking to me.

"Meaning he didn't spin out, and he never went for his brakes."

I said, "Maybe the bike went over without him."

This was my first alternative theory. He had looked down at the bike and hated it for bearing my name. So he pushed it off in anger and walked home without it.

Yeah. That could happen.

He said, "Not a chance."

I said, "But he's not here anywhere. Right?"

"It's a big ocean, ma'am."

I'm not used to being a ma'am. I don't think I make a very good ma'am. Don't you have to be years older than me to be a ma'am?

I said, "How can you be so sure he didn't push it off?"

He said, "He couldn't push it from the road. It's too far. It'd just stop and fall over."

"Walked it to the edge and pushed it."

Alternative theories were important. He didn't get that.

"Then there would have been footprints."

"Oh. Right."

"Has he been depressed lately that you know of?"

"You never know what someone else is feeling."

Which is true. In the most generic sense. I hardly knew James. Maybe he liked getting his heart torn out, thrown on the ground, and stomped on. You never know.

The gas tank was such a mangled mess you couldn't read my name anymore. Thank God. So they never had to know I killed somebody who loved me that much.

FOUR

Okay, So It's Weird

James was just getting in from work when I caught him. In fact, he was still sitting on his motorcycle in the driveway. Until he cut the motor, he didn't seem to hear me calling him. Then, when he did, he looked surprised. More than surprised, actually. Stunned.

I thought, Is that so weird? That I should go over and talk to him?

But then I knew the answer. Yes. It's very weird.

Because I never had before. Never. Not once, in four years. Well, two. I couldn't very well have gone over and talked to him while he was in the Air Force.

I suppose I could have written to him more than twice.

Anyway, my point is that he always sought me out. Always. I never called to him. I never said, Wait. James. Don't go away. Until now, when I needed something.

It's always about you, isn't it? That's actually what went through my head at that moment. I pushed those words away again. After all, they were Randy's. It was something Randy had said about me once, in an angry moment.

Of course, I was sure it wasn't true. Now I'm not sure of anything.

James was straddling the bike. He had his helmet braced against one thigh. With my name between his legs. That's just too weird. Rocking the bike ever so slightly from side to side.

I said, "Something I want to ask you." I said, "I just sort of . . . need a . . . date."

James sat up taller on the bike. "I'm your man," he said.

I felt a desperate need for a disclaimer. But I really had none. There is never an attorney around when you need one. I should put one on retainer for life in general.

I said, "It's just a onetime thing, though."

He said, "That's one more time than you've ever offered me before."

I said, "I don't know, though. I feel funny about it. Like I'm using you."

I guess I thought if we really clarified that I was using him, then it would be okay that I was using him.

He said, "Use me. I'm begging you."

That seemed like enough clarification. No lawyers required.

I looked past him to his house, and I wondered again how he ended up back in this same rented house after two years away. I'd wondered that before. So, a thought out of place, I guess, but there I was wondering it again.

He must have sublet it. I'd always half wanted to ask him why. But it's so self-explanatory, really. Why ask when some part of you already knows?

He wrote me a letter nearly every week while he was away. I wrote him twice in all. Maybe I said that already.

Five or ten minutes after I went back into the house I looked out the window and there he still was. Straddling the bike in his driveway. Rocking it ever so slightly back and forth. My name between his legs.

Journal Entry

```
Day I'm writing this: Twenty-seven
    days after "The Day"
Day I'm writing about: "The Day"
```

It's not the easiest thing in the world, telling a faceless emergency dispatcher over the telephone that you've misplaced James Stewart. You will inevitably be required to follow with something like, "That's right. James Stewart. Like the movie actor."

If you're really unlucky, like I was, the dispatcher will say, "But not *the* James Stewart."

Which is a ridiculous statement. Because *the* James Stewart is dead. It's a statement that gave me a little insight into James's world.

Maybe it's not such a wonderful life.

"*The* James Stewart is dead," I said to the dispatcher. Hoping they weren't both.

She said, "Oh, that's right. He is, isn't he? What a

shame, too. He was so good in *It's a Wonderful Life*. I love that movie. No accidents reported along that stretch. No motorcycle accidents in the county in the last twenty-four hours."

I didn't know what to do. I didn't know if I should call back.

I said, "Should I call back?"

She said, "If you want to report him missing, you'll have to call back day after tomorrow morning. But leave your name and number anyway. If we get an unidentified motorcycle accident victim, we'll want to contact you."

Not three hours later, there were two uniformed Highway Patrol officers. Knocking on my door. Just standing there, looking at me. Like they knew it was me or something. Like I had a big sign on my forehead.

And I swear to God I knew.

Later I backtracked. Told myself, and others, all kinds of stories. I was a veritable fountain of alternative theories. But just in that moment I had the distinct sensation that life as I had known it was over.

And, by the way, the journal thing is just to keep Dr. Grey happy. No way I would do a fool thing like this on my own. Believe me.

Journal Entry

Day I'm writing this: Twenty-eight days after "The Day"

Day I'm writing about: Two days after "The Day"

I've been through a few phases. There was this strange, brief no-man's-land where I reasoned there was still time to save myself. Because nobody had to know. This was evidenced by the fact that the Highway Patrol let me walk away free. They didn't know. They figured I'd been nice to the guy, been a decent friend, and he'd done this crazy thing anyway. Only Randy knew.

So I called Randy and told him that James had skidded out on a turn. Told him the tire tracks chronicled the whole sad, blameless story. Clear cognizance of guilt, when you cover up the crime. But covered up it was. Now nobody had to know.

My smoke screen didn't last long.

The phone blasted me out of sleep. I hadn't been dreaming. I hadn't had a dream in days.

I jumped for the phone.

I said, into it, "James?"

Randy said, "You thought it was James?"

Randy.

I said, "It could be James."

He said, "Theresa—"

"Stop talking, okay? Why are you even calling me?"

He said, "What, I can't call you anymore?"

I said, "I think it would be better if you didn't."

I'm the shooter, you're the gun. Stay out of my hands.

He said, "Ever?"

I said, "Yeah. Pretty much ever."

He said, "Okay, but before I hang up . . . I take it they still haven't found the body."

I wanted to ask if that was really why he called. I never did.

I just said, "Right, they still haven't." It was easier that way.

He said, "But it might be good for you to accept that they will."

I said, "I don't think James would do a thing like that."

He said, "You hardly knew him."

I said, "He was a solid guy. You know? I can't feature it on him."

He said, "Theresa. By your own admission he was a relative stranger."

"It still seems out of character," I said.

Then, after I hung up, I realized I'd just admitted James did not spin out on a curve. Which Randy probably knew anyway.

All is discovered, I thought.

But there was nothing I could do to change that. So I went back to bed.

FIVE

No More High School. Ever.

James took me to the party on the back of his motorcycle. Even though it was barely a mile away. I suppose we could have walked if we'd wanted to. But we didn't want to. We wanted to come roaring in and impress the hell out of everybody. I wanted him to park the bike where everybody would read my name on the gas tank. I wanted Randy to be sick with jealousy.

By the time we got there, I felt like I was about to throw up.

The inside of the barn was fixed up in the most natural way possible. Actually, maybe "fixed up" is the wrong way to put it. It's just that normally, because there are no horses, there's no hay or straw. So Frieda had some of the guys borrow a pickup and go out and get some. So, that was pretty much the whole motif. Simple. Hay and straw. On the barn floor. In the stalls. The cool thing about it was this: every surface became a seating area. Just get comfortable any way you please.

Randy and Rachel weren't there yet. I sat on the straw with James and tried to tell myself they'd never show. The whole thing had just been a sick joke. Nothing that terrible was about to happen to me.

Meanwhile I glanced obsessively at the barn door. About two times per second. More often than most people blink.

I think James noticed, but he kindly said nothing.

"Want me to get you a drink?" he asked. When he needed to say something. And I guess nothing else was floating around wanting to be said.

"Um. No. I don't, really. Drink." That just sat on the straw for a moment. While James was nice enough not to contradict me. I said, "That one time you saw me drunk was totally an exception to the rule. I hate drinking. I think it's stupid. I was just upset that night."

"How 'bout a soda or something?"

"Yeah. Okay. Thanks."

I looked around while he was gone. Well, not gone exactly. The drinks were waiting in a series of big picnic coolers in a far corner of the barn. There were only about ten people here. We were too early. We should have come fashionably late.

A girl I barely knew from school slid by and bumped me on the shoulder. When I looked over, she gave me a sly thumbs-up. I think I mostly returned an ignorant, questioning stare. I had no idea what she was trying to tell me. She flipped her head in the direction of James at the coolers.

Oh. Right. James.

I smiled and nodded. Wondering if it was painfully obvious that I couldn't even focus on James. I looked over my shoulder at him. Trying to see if he was really thumbs-up material. Maybe just because he was older. But it wasn't just that, I decided while I was trying to see him with new eyes. In purely objective terms, he was good-looking. I mean, if you divided people up into categories of good-looking, he'd be in a flattering category. I just wasn't attracted to him. The whole world was like a big black hole waiting for Randy's face to come along and fill it. Randy's face was like a drug to me. Something I needed. Something I got very edgy without. James had a face, but it didn't fill that craving.

I caught a whiff of someone's cigarette smoke.

"Oh my God, can you please take that outside!" I yelled. Before I even checked to see if it was someone I knew well enough to yell at. It wasn't. And then I felt bad because I yelled. You can do that with friends. They won't take it the wrong way.

This guy I didn't even know said, "I'm not going to set the straw on fire. If there's a spark I can always stamp it out."

"It's not the straw," I said. More politely. "I don't want it in my lungs."

"I got a right to smoke."

James appeared at my left shoulder. "Want me to take care of this for you?" Very much the gentleman. It was an offer I almost wanted to take him up on. I'm not used to chivalry, and I almost wanted to take it for a test-drive. But I like to fend for myself.

"Let me try logic for a minute," I said to James. Then to the idiot with the cancer stick, "Remember the first thing they taught us about rights in school? Your right to swing your fist ends where the other guy's nose begins? Well, your right to smoke your cigarette ends where my lungs begin. If you can keep your smoke out of my lungs I'll defend to the death your right to kill yourself. But I don't want to die. So I'll ask more nicely this time. Please will you take it outside?"

He sighed. Rose dramatically to his feet. Took it outside.

"Nice," James said.

"Thank you," I said.

Then I looked up to see Randy and Rachel walk in. Holding hands. The world collapsed on itself like a house of cards. Not one freaking building left standing.

I took hold of James's hand. He looked over and smiled at me. More than a little surprised.

I guess I need to cut to the chase here. There were other segments of the party, other horrible moments. But in the great scheme of things, they don't really matter. This matters.

Sometime around eleven or so, Randy and Rachel ended up in a stall. They weren't the first or the last. But it happened.

Now, I don't want to give a wrong impression of the whole stall experience. They only have half doors. Anybody could walk right up to one and look right over the door. So it wasn't quite the same as going off into a bedroom and locking the door. But close. Something was going on in there. Maybe not everything. But something.

Randy looked back over his shoulder at me on the way in. I'm not sure what I saw on his face. Maybe regret. Or even longing. It was hard to read.

I was just about to ask James to take me home when he took hold of my hand and led me into the stall right next door to you-know-who. He closed the door behind us, then smiled. Put a finger to my lips.

"I know we're doing all this to make him jealous," he whispered. "But it's okay."

I noticed that my mouth was open. Literally. That thing about someone's mouth hanging open can actually happen. "How can that be okay?"

"Well. It got you to go out with me. Anything that gets you to go out with me is good. When you get to know me more, you'll see. I'll treat you a lot better than he ever did."

Up to this point I might have sworn my stomach couldn't hurt more or drop lower. But I would have been wrong. It was like James opened a window and let me look into his mind. Not a pretty picture. He thought this was going to be a real thing between us. He thought I'd see that he was better. And that would be that. I guess in a weird sort of way I could follow his logic. We *should* want to be with the person who treats us well. That *should* be true. We *should* function that way. We just don't.

Why don't we?

"Want to make him *really* jealous?" James asked. We were sitting on the straw by this time. He moved his face in close. "Is this okay? If I kiss you?"

63

"How will that make him jealous? He can't see us."

"I guess you'll have to make a lot of noise about it."

So, I look back to that moment. I see it as the real heart of where things began to go wrong. Not that things weren't *pretty* wrong before that. But after it, things were *really* wrong. Unprecedented-crazy wrong. So wrong that I ended up stretched out on my back with James on top of me, his hands all interwoven with mine above our heads, kissing. And me calling out his name. About three or four times. Before it hit me. Maybe he didn't realize this was still all part of the Make Randy Jealous crusade. Maybe he'd gotten carried away, lost track of all that, and thought I was calling his name because he was doing great with me. He seemed carried away. But even then, after wondering about that, I had no idea what to do about it.

"I need to stop for a minute," I said.

We sat up.

"What's wrong?" he asked.

I had no idea where to begin. We were past the point of no return and there was nothing I could say without hurting him. And I didn't want to hurt James. Have I made that clear already?

I heard the door of the next stall slam. I looked up to see the top of Randy's head go by the door. He purposely did not look in.

"Are you okay?" James again. "Do you need something? Fresh air? Something to drink?"

"Yeah. Maybe a glass of water."

"I'll be right back."

"I'll be outside getting some air."

"Good idea," he said.

I'd barely been outside long enough to take my first breath when Randy came up from behind me. Startling me.

"I'm sorry I scared you," he said, "but we need to talk."

"Where's Rachel?"

"I gave her my car and told her to go home."

"How will you get home?"

"Hopefully with you."

"I didn't drive. I came here with James."

"We could walk."

"Randy. I came here with James. That would be kind of cold."

"*I* did it for *you*. I sent Rachel home. Look, I was wrong. How many different ways do I have to say it? I was wrong. I want us back together. Please. We belong together. What do I have to do? I'll do anything."

I looked into his eyes and folded.

Another moment good for looking back on. Or bad for it. As the case may be. I could have held firm. But I didn't. I saw the emotion in his eyes and turned to jelly.

He pulled me in to kiss me. I let him.

It was . . . everything. It was like a key you put into a lock, and it fits, and the whole world just opens wide. It was the very thing. The ticket. The only answer. There was nothing else like it. There never would be. There never could be. There was only one Randy. This was the only kiss in the world.

I'm not sure how long we'd been kissing when I remembered there was such a thing as James. I'd like to at least pretend that it returned to my mind all on its own. But even that would be giving me too much credit. The truth of the matter is that I heard a motorcycle start up. That's what made me think of James.

"How long have we been out here?" I asked.

"I don't know. Why?"

"James went to get me a glass of water."

And, of course, he'd had plenty of time to come back with it by now.

I am a very, very horrible person. I am beyond redemption.

I ran around looking for him. Pretending there were lots of motorcycles parked at Frieda's that night. That the odds were good I had heard someone else's bike entirely.

I ran into Frieda, who said, "Poor James. I've never seen anybody so upset."

I said, "This is totally your fault. You told me to invite him."

I know. I'm a horrible person. I have apologized for that remark since. Five times at last count. Which doesn't make it even remotely okay.

"I didn't tell you to ditch him and go back to Randy halfway through the party."

There she had me. That last part had been my own unique idea.

I stood for a few minutes in the spot where his motorcycle had been parked. But I could not make it miraculously reappear.

Things are so easy to do, so hard to undo. I made a mental note of that.

Journal Entry

Day I'm writing this: Twenty-nine
    days after "The Day"
Day I'm writing about: Five days
    after "The Day"

I tried ditching school. Thought it would be easy. After all, there were only three days left. I called the principal's office. Made an arrangement for Frieda to come in and pick up my diploma. Told them I had to regrettably miss graduation. A regrettable case of other obligations. All of which I regretted.

Like they hadn't already heard how I killed a guy.

Then I realized that my locker needed to be cleaned out.

Now, I guess it stands to reason that Frieda could have done that, too. But I was so heavily into my life-in-a-suit-of-armor phase that I didn't want anyone going through my stuff. Not even my best friend. And I'm not sure why, because I don't even know that there was anything terribly personal in my locker. But there could have been. And everything was personal. Suddenly.

I wore sunglasses in the hall and cleaned out my own locker.

I didn't see any of my actual friends. Just a bunch of familiar faces.

They recognized me behind my sunglasses. Imagine that.

I unexpectedly magically opened up a path through the crowded hallway like Moses parting the Red Sea.

I looked at their faces. It wasn't condemnation I saw there.

It was . . . I hate to even use the word. But it's the only way to say it.

It was awe.

As if I have a right to kill guys using love as a murder weapon. As if that's somehow stunningly cool.

I wanted to scream at them. Tell them I did *not* have the right to do what I did to James. No one did.

I got out as fast as I could. More to the point, I kept silent. The only really wise move I'd made in as long as I can remember.

Journal Entry _____

```
Day I'm writing this: Thirty days
    after "The Day"
Day I'm writing about: Three days
    after "The Day"
```

It was a Tuesday night. James had been gone since Saturday.

I moved out of the denial phase. Set up shop in bargaining.

I was lying in bed. Which was nothing special. That's mostly what I'd been doing. Lying in bed.

And I started missing him.

No, that's not even right, to say I started. I didn't start. I just kind of joined it in progress, zero to a hundred percent while I wasn't even paying attention. It wasn't there, then it was. And it was big, too. Big and mean.

I was stretched out on my back and thought about

that night in the barn with him. At Frieda's. Really thought about it for the first time.

Here I'd already lived that night, but this was the first time I honestly thought about it.

Then I stopped thinking about it and started feeling it.

Also for the first time.

My arms were out and back, behind my head, palms up. Feeling his fingers engaged with mine. Feeling his hands in my hands. Gently pinning them down, moving together without hands.

His lips on my neck. The tip of his tongue.

I threw my head back to cry out. But this time I wasn't talking to Randy. This time there was no Randy. Almost like there never had been. Definitely like there never would be again.

I couldn't even feel James move with me, because that would just have been too much. Too intensely personal. I might have exploded. As it was, I felt every nerve ending exposed. I felt skinless. But it was a pleasurable exposure.

I felt it.

And it had very little to do with lust. In fact, there was something strangely pure about it. Like religion.

If I had felt it any more strongly, I might have cracked like a china cup. It was like a pressure inside me, like an old steam boiler, and I just lay there hoping it would hold. Hoping *I* would hold.

And then I knew I'd had all this, and I hadn't even been there to notice. I'd been so possessed by my own anxiety over Randy that I'd been absent from what I now saw as a significant event. I had to notice now, after the fact. Try to re-create what had once been placed right in my hand.

You know what it was like? It was like I finally looked up and saw the whale.

My best revelations have a bad habit of stumbling home a few hours after curfew.

I made this deal with God. Even though we'd never spoken before. Like the man said about atheists in foxholes. Or, actually, about the absence of them.

I said, Walk him through the door in one piece. Right now, okay? I know, that would be a miracle. But that's what you do, right? Aren't you the guy in charge of miracles?

Okay, so give him back now. Pull strings, do what you have to do, I don't care.

And here's what I'll do for my part in the deal. I will never, ever, as long as I live, fail to appreciate his goodness again.

I mean, if I live to be 100 and he's still alive and kicking at the ripe old age of 104, I swear not for one minute of all those years together will I take for granted the blessing of James.

What do you say, God? Have we got a deal?

The following morning James washed up onto William Randolph Hearst State Beach in San Simeon.

That was the first day I shaved my head.

Journal Entry

Day I'm writing this: Thirty-one
    days after "The Day"
Day I'm writing about: Today

This morning I woke up sweating. It wasn't light yet, so I sat up in bed in the dark. And sat and sat. But nothing changed. Nothing ever changes.

So I left a voice-mail message telling Dr. Grey that I'm leaving myself.

It went like this:

"Dr. Grey.

"I know this is going to come as a shock to me, but I am leaving me. Perhaps I'll say I could not have seen this coming, but truthfully things have been wrong between me for some time. Time heals and I'm sure in time I'll build a new life without me.

"Please cancel my regular appointments, as I will be nowhere around.

"Oh. Did I mention that this is Theresa?"

After I hung up the phone, I sat some more. But like I said before, nothing ever changes.

I left a note for my absentee father. Then I started to pack.

PART TWO

ONE

Disdain Gets Them Every Time

Theresa Anne Eagan lay on the hot metal of her car hood; the sun baked her face and outstretched arms. When she raised a cigarette to her lips and took a long draw, the heat of it in her lungs completed the package, nicely pushing that envelope of discomfort.

She purposely parked here—in a dirt lot, up a hill from the paved employee parking—because it was not easily seen from anywhere. Close enough to the Roman Pool to hear the guides deliver canned, well-practiced farewells to their tour groups, but only as a one-way awareness. Like a fly on a wall. A hot fly on a hot wall.

A voice startled her slightly, a close voice. But startled her only on the inside.

"Annie."

She betrayed nothing of her surprise, didn't twitch or

raise her head. In fact, she didn't even open her eyes. "I'd have to guess that's Art."

His voice again, from beside her left arm. "There's a party down in the guide trailer. You should come down."

She didn't respond. Just took another hot draw.

"Todd's birthday. There's cake."

"What kind of cake?"

"Chocolate with chocolate frosting."

"First significant thing you've said all morning. I'll be down in a while."

"Why do you come up here? You don't want anybody to know you smoke?"

"Everybody knows I smoke."

The diesel roar of a tour bus coming around the circle, headed back down the hill. The metallic complaint of its gears, the stench of exhaust.

"Then why do you come up here?"

"To be alone."

"Oh, right. I get it. I can take a hint."

Annie opened her eyes. Raised her head to address him. As if taking him in for the first time. "Could've fooled me."

"You shouldn't lie in the sun so much."

She lay back again and closed her eyes. Took another draw and then let her arm droop off to the side, dangling in the air beside the hood of her hot car. Hoping he would go away on his own.

"I mean, it's a great tan. But you're gonna get skin cancer."

"Promise?"

Art laughed, a short, nervous bark. "You say the weird-est things. I get to guard your Tour One next."

"You say that like it's a good thing."

"It is. I love to listen to you talk. I love to look at you. In fact, I think I love *you*." He said this last with a flour-ish, dropping to one knee and taking her hand. She pulled it away. Turned her head and frowned at him from behind her sunglasses.

"If you really loved me you wouldn't make me talk it. You'd trade and let me guard." The prized guard position involved very little work. Just walk in the back and be sure the group stayed together. Which explained why it was so prized.

"If that would improve my image in your beautiful eyes."

"You're not going to give me your guard, Art. Don't toy with me."

"It's yours."

She sat up. Raised her sunglasses and looked at him full-on. She did seem to like him a bit better already. He drew to his feet, a patch of brown dirt on the knee of his gray polyester uniform pants.

She noticed he held a piece of cake in a napkin. He noticed her notice.

"Want some?"

"Yeah." She reached her hand out for it, but he drew it back.

"Just a bite. If you want a whole piece you have to come down to the trailer."

"Okay, a bite, then."

"Okay, but it's crumbly. It'll get all over. Here."

He held it up to her face, and she reached out and took a bite, no hands. "One more," she said with her mouth still full.

"No. You have to come down."

"Damn it, Art."

"A deal's a deal," he said. "Wait till I tell Todd I had you eating out of my hand." And he disappeared down the hill.

She shook her head and lay back down. Drew again on the cigarette. But it was depressingly close to the filter now, so she took the pack out of her blazer pocket and lit another from it. She didn't need chocolate cake that badly. She just needed to be alone.

But at least she didn't have to talk the next tour. Already the day was looking up.

"Welcome to Hearst San Simeon State Historical Monument. A place William Randolph Hearst called La Cuesta Encantada. The Enchanted Hill. My name is Arthur Friedman, and I'll be your guide this afternoon. That lovely young woman with the modern haircut at the back of the tour is my partner, Annie Stewart. If you have a problem as the tour goes along or need a translation brochure, drop back and talk to Annie. I envy you that already."

Annie stood behind the fifty-two tourists at the Hello Spot, smiling behind her sunglasses in a way she hoped looked interested.

Art, unlike most guides, gave the same tour every time. And she was already bored with it. And she found his stridency enervating. But at least she could follow along in silence, thinking her own thoughts. Which, just at the moment, were no more significant or complicated than, Yo, Art, if they don't speak English, how are they supposed to understand that I can give them a translation brochure?

Meanwhile his voice droned in the background of her heavy, nearly immobile thoughts. Asking for no flash photography, for the group to stay on the tour mats and touch nothing except the concrete or iron handrails.

A burst of laughter from the crowd, which meant he had just used his usual line, "I'm the only art in the Castle you can touch."

Then the group was moving, teeming around both sides of the fountain like water flowing uphill.

Up the stairs, then right to C Terrace, where Annie leaned on the cast concrete railing and stared out over William Randolph Hearst State Beach.

And hoped briefly that nobody would need anything.

Just underneath the main terrace, on the steps to the left of Sekhmet, the ancient Egyptian sculpture, Annie heard Leander's voice for the first time that day. She knew just where he was standing, from experience. Knew his usual Day Security post, on the main terrace, at the foot of the ridiculously ornate Main House, in the shade of a Hearst-imported magnolia tree.

She moved partway up the stairs, stopping with a view of both the terrace and the tour group below. And looked at Leander. Art had a long, complex spiel about Sekhmet, so she was in no hurry.

But to her disappointment, Leander was talking to his girlfriend from Gardening.

Annie didn't like his girlfriend. Not because she was his girlfriend so much, but because she didn't treat him well. Because he looked at her with those gleaming, unguarded brown eyes, not knowing that she described her relationship with him as "no exclusive thing" when out of his earshot. Annie regularly wrestled with an urge to tell him, though that was clearly not her place.

The Tour One directly in front of hers cleared the area on its way into the Assembly Room, leaving Leander and the girl alone on the concrete terrace. He grabbed her and began to dance. It looked almost like a waltz: long, stately strides that swirled them around and around and, at one point, brought them dangerously close to the fishpond surrounding the main terrace fountain.

He was a little smaller than she always remembered him, and a little darker. And it wasn't his features exactly, but the animation of them. The way he smiled at that girl. Which she did not deserve. On one wide sweep he saw Annie and waved to her over his girlfriend's shoulder. She smiled and nodded rather than wave back, because she didn't want the group to know her attention was fully elsewhere.

Then the waltz turned into a broadly executed mock tango, their arms outstretched and cheeks pressed together. Annie couldn't help but smile, despite her ambivalence.

Leander stopped briefly, leaned back, picked a flower—first glancing around to convince himself that nobody but Annie was watching—and held it to the face of the girl, who opened her mouth to receive it. Their cheeks pressed together again, the flower clenched tightly in her teeth.

Annie became aware of Art glancing sideways at her as he spoke.

Art finished his speech, and the group poured around Sekhmet like herded cattle, anxious to take a break in the shade. Leander's girlfriend ran back to her work. The tourists sat on the hard concrete benches and fanned themselves and smoked and looked up at the Castle in wonder or revulsion or more likely both. And Art talked. And Annie sidled into the shade next to Leander, nearly shoulder to shoulder.

"Hey."

"Hey, Annie. You didn't see me pick that flower."

"What flower?"

"Thanks. You got lucky today. Two guards."

"Art gave me his."

"Get outta town! No way."

"I'm telling you."

"He's just a nice guy, or what?"

"More like the 'or what,' I think."

Leander laughed.

And then Annie had nothing more to say. It happened this way. Because she didn't know him. He just reminded her of someone, and yet he wasn't that someone. Not at close range. And because she had never been good at talking for real anyway.

So they just stood in the shade.

When the group massed into a bulky line headed for the Main House, Annie took her place bringing up the rear. Just before she pulled level with the house, just as the last tourist's back disappeared through the cool concrete doorway, she looked over her shoulder.

There he still was, standing in the shade, hands clasped and dangling in front of him. And he smiled at her.

You could do better, she told him in her head.

She didn't mean he could do her. Just that he could do better.

Her hands slid into her blazer pockets, touching the pack of cigarettes and a pile of loose change. She pulled out a quarter and, turning fully back to face the terrace, levered her thumb under it and flipped it into the air. Praying it would make it all the way to the pond. Because he was watching. As it arced end over end, the aim and distance looking good so far, she made a wish.

I hope Leander doesn't get hurt.

The quarter landed in the water with a satisfying plunk.

He shot her a thumbs-up. "Three points," he called.

"I hope I get my wish."

"You will," he said. "I'm sure you will."

He smiled.

She smiled.

She ducked through the concrete archway into the Assembly Room.

She spent her day off at the Cove, as the locals called William Randolph Hearst State Beach. Sunning until she was too hot to bear it, then dipping into the ocean and swimming out beyond the waves until her temperature came back down. Shaking her head as if to whip water out of her hair, purely out of force of habit, then lying back down on her towel, feeling the drops of salt water evaporate one by one. Drinking Coronas and smoking too much.

Heaven, until Art showed up. Which he did about one time in four, because she was here regularly enough that it paid to cruise by and look for her car.

"Mind if I join you?"

"Do I get a choice?"

She could hear and feel him sit in the sand at her left side. "Which do you think will get you first? Melanoma or lung cancer?"

"I don't bet on the races, I just watch them."

A beautiful moment of silence. She sat up to take a long slug of beer. Opened her eyes to the small commercial fishing boats anchored offshore, the pier on her left, with San Simeon Acres, the motel zone, beyond. And to her right the Point, a high wooded peninsula of Hearst land. For the moment, gloriously undeveloped.

"Lot of speculation about you in the guide trailer."

"Don't you guys have anything better to do?"

"No. It's what you get for not telling anybody anything about you. People make stuff up. You should hear some of the things."

She wiped sweat from her brow. Ran her hand through her hair. Again, force of habit. It wasn't even long enough to lie flat. Lay back again and closed her eyes. "Okay, I'll bite. Tell me some of the things."

"That you just got out of jail."

"Good one."

"True?"

"No."

"That you almost died of cancer, and that's why your hair's so short. From the chemo. But then somebody pointed out that you have to take a physical for this job."

"Is that all?"

"I've barely scratched the surface. Most people think you're gay."

"That figures."

"Why does it figure?"

"I have short hair, and they don't happen to see me with anybody."

"*Are* you gay?"

"Well, not at the moment, Art. But keep pushing at me. It's not out of the question."

Another beautiful silence. She could feel him shift around. When she looked over, he'd settled back onto his elbows. Wearing cutoff jeans and no shirt. Skinny and pale. She hoped he was smart enough to wear number forty-five sunblock.

"I knew you weren't. Because I see the way you look at Leander. Rumor has it you've got a thing for him."

She didn't bother to answer.

"*Do* you have a thing for him?"

"No."

"Well, even so. If you were gay you wouldn't have a guy's name tattooed on your chest."

She reflexively rolled onto her stomach.

"Who is this James?"

"Just a guy I used to know."

"Where is he now?"

"Nowhere."

"Nowhere?"

"Or everywhere. Depending on how you want to look at it."

"You give such elliptical answers. It's really hard to ask you questions."

"And yet you just keep doing it."

He jumped to his feet. "Right. Sorry."

Before he was two steps away she called after him, "Wait. Art. I'm sorry. I didn't mean to hurt your feelings."

"No, you're right. I should leave you alone."

"Art, it's okay. I'm sorry. Really. The last thing I want to do is hurt your feelings."

He waved over his shoulder as he walked off down the beach.

She lay on her stomach a moment with her head in her hands. It didn't work. It never worked. Maybe it never would. You had to hurt them to keep them away, and if you didn't keep them away, they'd get hurt. She'd tried it from just about every angle, and it seemed there was no way out.

In the morning she sat with Todd in the fog, at a picnic table on the dirt hill behind the guide trailer. He gave her half of his cinnamon roll.

Normally the hilltop rose above the summer fog. Which is why Hearst's father camped on this site, she'd grown sick to death of saying. But this morning the fog hovered at hilltop level, cool and welcome.

Todd didn't talk much, an appealing quality.

She said, "Happy belated birthday, by the way."

He said, "Thank you." Apparently surprised and flattered.

They sat quietly another minute or two, and Annie finished her sweet roll and wiped her sticky fingers on a napkin. And looked at Todd. She wore her sunglasses, even in the fog. Maybe the better to look at Todd.

He was big and broad-shouldered and blond and handsome. More to the point, he was quiet and polite, which figured into her attraction to him. And that represented a problem to Annie, who knew she could take him apart if she were to let those thoughts pull her all the way into actions.

She took out a cigarette.

Then Art stuck his head out the back trailer door and said, "Hey, Annie. Leander's on the front patio. I figured you'd want to know."

And some part of her, a part she'd yet to acknowledge, felt relieved to see Art. As if it had been in question whether she ever would again. And even though none of that made any genuine sense, it felt real enough to cause her to overlook the fact that he was teasing her in a not entirely pleasant or well-meaning way.

"Art. Sorry about yesterday."

"It's okay."

"No, it's not."

"It's not a big deal, okay?"

He disappeared again.

And she thought, Thank God. He's here in one piece. I can stop thinking about that. Though she hadn't been thinking about it. Not consciously. She tried to strike a match, noticing her hands shake slightly.

Todd watched in silence, his head tilted slightly to one side. Then he took the matches from her hand and lit the cigarette for her. She could easily have touched his hand to steady the flame, but she didn't.

"I shouldn't do this. I'm helping you kill yourself." A pause, during which he handed back the matches. "He means well."

"Who, Art?"

"Yeah. Art. It's just, when he likes somebody, he's kind of loud about it."

"Strident."

"Yeah. Strident."

"He's okay. Bit of a pest. But I don't actually dislike him or anything. I'm just trying to make him stay back a few steps. For his own sake." Then she talked over the moment to avoid questions. "Tell me something, Todd." His head took on that slight tilt again. Unlike her—unlike most people—he watched and listened. "What in God's name do you guys see in me? Honestly."

"Well, it's not *all* the guys. Just a group of them. Actually, it's mostly Art and that whole little group of college trainees. Well, it's most of them. You're right."

"And you."

"What gave me away?"

"Art did. Besides, you gave me half your cinnamon roll."

"Yeah, that I did. Well. You're beautiful."

"I'm also nearly bald, thirty pounds underweight, and

hard to get along with. Plus, how do you know I'm even old enough to be legal?"

"You couldn't have gotten a job here if you weren't eighteen. There's just something about you, I guess."

"Like what?"

"Like an attitude thing. You're an enigma."

"I dismiss you, so I'm an enigma."

"Yeah. I think that's it. You want nothing to do with us. And that's attractive."

There's plenty I want to do with you, she thought, and just for a moment that thought swept her aside, like a wave that hits you hard as you wade out. Moves you a few yards back before you can get to your feet again. But she pushed the thought away.

"Who knew disdain was such an aphrodisiac?"

"Best one there is," he said, and they sat quietly for a time.

The sun broke through the fog, warming her scalp.

Todd said, "So *do* you have a thing for that Day Security guy?"

"Who, Leander?"

"Yeah. Leander."

"No."

"You're always looking at him."

"He just reminds me of somebody. I just keep looking at him, thinking how he reminds me of a guy I used to know."

"But it's not, like, a romantic thing."

"No."

"So us guide guys still have a shot with you?"

Annie laughed, blowing smoke out her nose. "Not a chance," she said.

TWO

By Her Fruits Ye Shall Know Her

Annie sat at the bar, staring straight ahead. Holding a cigarette in her right hand, which was rested on her ear, smoke curling up against her head. Watching herself in the bar mirror. In her periphery she saw Todd come in.

He sat on the bar stool to her right.

Sunday night. The place was quiet. Sparsely populated. Comfortable.

"Annie."

"Hey, Todd."

"You shaved your head again."

She watched his face in the mirror without comment. Saw his hand come up, as if to touch her bare scalp. Hesitated there a moment.

"May I?"

She only shrugged.

He ran his hand over the smooth skin of her scalp. More than once. And she held still and allowed it. Reacting slightly to his touch—to being touched at all, by anyone—but careful to keep that to herself.

"It's so smooth. Just like a baby's butt."

"So the more you keep doing that, the more that makes you a pedophile and a pervert. Right?"

"Well, when you put it like that."

He brought his hand down. Faced ahead. Looked into the mirror and caught her eye. The bartender looked questioningly to Todd, prepared to take an order.

"What are you drinking, Annie?" Todd asked.

"Tequila."

"Can I buy you another one?"

"Sure you can."

He ordered another round for her, a Michelob for himself.

They fell silent for a time. She was hoping he wouldn't comment on her age. So far the bartender hadn't bothered to wonder. At least not out loud.

"Thanks for the drink."

"It looks good on you."

"What does?"

"The skinhead thing. It works on you."

Annie let out a breath, hard and audibly. Rolled her eyes and set her head down on one folded arm. Snubbed her cigarette into the ashtray without looking.

"Was that not the right thing to say?"

She came upright. Shook her head slightly. Rubbed her face, her eyes. Then remembered she was still wearing makeup. Looked at the damage in the mirror and realized she didn't care.

"That is just, like, so far from the intention."

"What's the intention?"

"I don't know. Kind of hard to explain. Not to be more attractive, that's for sure. I guess it's my version of a hair shirt. No pun intended. Plus, if it really is beauty you guys are looking for, it's my best shot at ugly."

"Not working. It's not your only kind of beauty."

"I have no idea what that means. But I'm not going to ask. Because you might tell me."

"There's something from the inside, too. Like a light."

"And you can actually see this through the basket I'm hiding it under?"

"Must be a pretty strong light."

A noisy couple spilled in the door. As if already drunk. Laughing and talking too loudly. Annie turned her head to see. Her stomach tightened. Todd glanced around, re-acting to whatever he'd just seen on her face. Seeing nothing odd, he looked back.

"What?"

"Nothing."

Silence. He didn't ask. And she appreciated the fact that he didn't ask, so she told him.

"I just don't like that girl."

"Isn't that the girl from Gardening?"

"Yeah."

"The one that dates Leander."

"Yes."

"Why don't you like her?"

"Who is she with now, Todd?"

"I don't know. I don't know that guy."

"Is it Leander?"

"No."

"Does that answer your question?"

He sipped his beer and chewed on that awhile in silence.

Meanwhile the girl and her date managed to destroy whatever silence may have been left to enjoy. The girl hit the jukebox, punched in three songs, and racked up a game of pool. The first song came up, blaring country and western.

Annie's jaw set more tightly. She lit another cigarette. Thought about leaving. But first she had to talk to Todd. She had to settle this thing with him once and for all. Because even if you don't openly encourage a guy, it still happens. It's still building up. It's all in what he's thinking, what he expects. Allows as a possibility.

But now she couldn't think, what with the bad music and the clack of pool balls and the voice of that girl grating at her.

Todd said, "Maybe they have an open thing."

"He adores her. He never looks at anybody but her."

"Okay. But even so. I mean, maybe she's an okay person. I mean, she could be nice. Just not be very . . . you know . . . monogamous. I mean, nice people can do things like that."

Annie massaged her forehead, took a long draw off her

cigarette, blowing the smoke out through her nose; she tried to erect an inner barrier against the noise and disturbance.

She said, "So many people will steal from work if it's only a pen."

Todd sat with that for a respectable length of time, then said, "I'm not sure what you're trying to tell me."

"A few days ago I was walking by the Roman Pool. Nobody else around. And one of the guys who's restoring the floor in there, he calls me in. Wants to give me a handful of the original Hearst gold floor tiles. I think he's trying to make me. 'Here,' he says. 'Nobody'll know. No big deal.'"

"What'd you do?"

"I didn't take them." Pause. "Want to know why not?"

"Yes. I do. Very much. I would really like to know anything about you that the other guys on the hill don't know."

She turned her head and looked directly at him for the first time since he'd come in. Right into his eyes. It seemed to alarm him slightly.

"Because if you take something you're a thief." She nursed the silence a moment. Downed the balance of her drink and silently signaled for another. "Sounds simple, but you'd be amazed how many people don't get it. They steal but they call themselves honest. They cheat on their spouses and lovers but they think they're good people. They lie but they'd never call themselves liars. Well, let me tell you something, Todd. . . ." She pointed toward him with her right hand, with her lit cigarette. He leaned away slightly. She looked into the mirror of his eyes and saw herself going too far. "You are what you do. That's what I'm trying to tell you. What we do defines us. However we behave, conduct our lives . . . that's real. The rest is just a story for publication."

She dropped her hand again. They sipped their drinks for a moment in silence.

Well, not silence. There was that damn music, that clacking of pool balls. The chatter and laughter of that girl she couldn't stand.

"Sorry," Todd said. "Didn't mean to hit a nerve."

"No, it's not your fault. It's my fault. Look, I'm gonna get out of here."

She tossed back the rest of her drink and slid, wobbly, to her feet. Made her way for the door fast and straight, as if to plow right through that other girl, causing the girl to jump out of the way.

Cool air hit her face as she strode out onto the dark sidewalk.

"Annie." Todd's voice behind her. Following her out. "Wait, Annie. Let me give you a lift home."

She waved him off without turning around.

"Annie. I don't think you should drive right now."

"I'm not driving. I just live right down there. In that trailer park right down the street there." He pulled level with her. "I'm just going to walk home and get some sleep."

"At least let me walk with you, then."

"I'm fine, Todd. I'm sorry. I'm just not good company tonight."

"It's late though, Annie, just let me walk with you. It's safer if I walk with you."

But it wasn't safe, not at all, and she knew it. If she opened the door of her trailer and he was right there with her. That would not be safe. She knew she might pull him in with her and lock the door behind them.

As they crossed in front of the bank, Annie slammed her left shoulder hard against a wooden post holding up the building's awning. Meant to walk right by it but misjudged and hit it hard and bounced off again. Stood feeling surprised and wounded, and Todd stopped. He came close and rubbed her shoulder gently.

"You okay?"

She purposely fell forward into his arms. Held him. Rested her head on his shoulder, close into the crook of his neck. And it must have startled him, because a second or two passed before he circled her with his arms.

He lifted her chin and tried to kiss her, but she pulled away.

"No, don't," she said.

She leaned back against the post that had stopped them in the first place. And pulled him back with her, against her. Apparently surprising him again.

"Just hold me," she said.

And he did, for a longish time. How long, she found herself unable to judge. His hands ran up and down her back, dipping a little too low each time, as if trying to sneak a border transgression past them both. But she had no intention of giving in to that. It would have been blissfully easy, but she couldn't. She knew she couldn't.

"I miss being held," she said. "Being touched. I'm lonely. There. Now you know something about me that the other guys don't."

"Come home with me," he said.

"I can't."

"Okay, I'll come home with you."

"No. I can't."

She pulled away and headed for home again. More slowly and carefully.

"You can't tell me you don't want to," he called.

She stopped, turned around. He looked lonely and small, standing on the dark sidewalk on Sunday night, alone. She felt sorry for him.

See? She'd already done him some harm.

"I didn't say I didn't want to. I said I wasn't going to. Oh my God. Don't you get it? I'm just trying to make everybody stay away. Just stay away."

She threw her hands up in frustration. Turned and walked steadily for home again.

A few steps later he appeared at her right. On the street side, the way a gentleman is told to walk with a woman.

"It's still safer if I walk you," he said.

She took his hand and held it as they walked. For the first time in as long as she could remember, she felt as if things were maybe okay. Or at least could be.

At the door of her trailer she kissed his cheek and did not invite him in, and he left without comment.

Sometime later that night, she was startled by a knock at the door. Her muscles jumped, spasmed the way they might in a dream about falling. She squeezed her eyes shut. The sweet thoughts of Todd, of anybody, a body, a touch, evaporated in the sure knowledge that all of those things lurked in dangerous proximity.

"Don't do this, Todd," she said. Quietly and out loud. "I had so much respect for you because you didn't do this. Don't screw it up now."

Another knock. But this time she was prepared.

She pulled on a robe, made her way through the dark hall without stubbing her toes, rested her hands on the door latch, and squeezed her eyes shut one more time.

She swung the door wide.

There on her dim porch, half illuminated by the corner streetlight, stood Frieda.

She looked at Frieda, and Frieda looked at her.

She had changed a little over the months, Annie noticed. Her hair had been done in a frizzier style, and her lips and nails, classically blood-red, looked almost dark purple in this limited light. Still nothing had been said.

Annie spoke first. Leaned through the door and addressed Frieda in a hushed tone, a near whisper. "What are you doing here?"

Frieda leaned in to meet her halfway, stage-whispering

in an obvious parody of Annie, "I was just about to ask you the same question. Why are we whispering?"

"It's late," Annie said, which wasn't why.

"Yeah, sorry about that. Who's Annie Stewart?"

"Oh. Well, that's kind of a long story."

Frieda's arms flew out wide, as if to take in every possible explanation. "I've got nothing but time."

Out of options, Annie conceded that she had best come in.

I'm doing this very well after all those tequilas, she thought as she stepped back from the doorway, allowed Frieda into her living room, closed the door behind them.

She turned back to Frieda, who said, "Boy, you're hammered. Huh?"

"How did you find me here?"

"Look at you. Not even peach fuzz."

For the second time that night, a smooth hand across the bare skin of her scalp.

"I was growing it out for a while. But sometimes I still—how did you *find* me here?"

"Well, honey, that's kind of a long story, too. Why don't we save long stories for the morning? You won't remember any of this tomorrow anyway."

"I'm not that drunk."

"Honey. I know you."

You don't, she thought. Nobody does. You knew Theresa. But she didn't say so, because it would sound like a hurtful thing to say. And because even Annie had to concede that she probably shared Theresa's lack of resistance to alcohol.

Frieda smiled suddenly and held her arms out. From force of habit and probably much more, Annie walked in. Frieda was a big, tall girl, and Annie's head rested comfortably on her shoulder, her face in the crook of her neck. Frieda held her.

It was every bit as comforting as embracing Todd, and a whole lot safer.

THREE

On Not Knowing Where

Annie woke early, for no discernible reason. She found her way to her kitchen in the half-light, her stomach queasy, eyes grainy, head a mess. Thirsty. More than anything else, thirsty. She stood naked in the dawn at her own sink, preparing to stoop to drink the grotesque, mineral-laden local tap water. Pulled a heavy glass mug down from the cupboard.

Dropped it on the linoleum at the sound of a voice.

It said, "Damn. You're skinny, aren't you?"

The cup landed hard on its base but did not break. The noise made Annie wince.

Then, still rattled, she fell back against the counter, hand to her chest, breathing hard and talking to her heart.

The lump on the living room sofa appeared to be, of all things, Frieda. The voice spoke again. "They say you can never be too thin or too rich. But you might be pushing the limits there, sweetie."

"Well, if it will make you happy," she said, her voice still ragged with breath, "I'll give away some of my money."

Frieda sat up, pulling the knit afghan around herself. "Sorry I startled you."

Annie put on a long flannel shirt and sat down on the coffee table next to the couch. Close enough to touch Frieda, but she didn't. "Frieda. What are you doing here?"

Frieda swept masses of hair off her face with both hands. "I was sleeping, but you put a stop to that."

"How did you get in?"

Frieda fixed her with a pitying look. "I told you you wouldn't remember last night."

"You did?"

"Absolutely."

"When did you tell me that?"

"Last night."

"Right. I guess I might have seen that one coming."

Her mind flickered back to the night before. Todd. She remembered sitting at the bar with him. Smoking and watching them both in the bar mirror. But what troubled her was what, if anything, took place in that big black hole of later in the evening.

Meanwhile Frieda told her to put on her clothes, she'd

buy her breakfast. But breakfast was the farthest thing from Annie's mind. And the farther it stayed from her stomach, the better.

They sat on the outdoor patio of Sebastian's Store and Coffee Bar in Old San Simeon. Annie sat with her back to the original Hearst warehouses, looking in the general direction of the Castle. Currently blissfully hidden in the early morning fog. Watching instead the old one-room schoolhouse and the flat brownness of the dry summer grass. Still very aware that the Castle was up there. Waiting for her. Whether she could see it or not.

Frieda's breakfast arrived, and Annie tried not to smell it. She asked the waitress if she had any buttermilk.

"That's not on the menu," was the reply.

"That wasn't the question," Annie said.

"I could ask the cook."

"Please do. Thank you."

"I wouldn't know what to charge for it."

"Make something up. Overcharge me. I really don't care."

The waitress disappeared, and Annie lit a cigarette. Inhaled deeply and felt the predictable sensation of queasiness. She'd known all along that the first cigarette of the morning would make her sicker, but it really wasn't optional.

She thought again about Todd. Maybe she should drive up the hill after this and talk to him. No, he was off today. She should call him. But she'd have to look up the number. Which meant she'd have to remember his last name. Damn it, she knew his last name. At one time she had. Hell, she saw it on the schedule every day. Why didn't she pay attention to these things?

Frieda waved her smoke away. "By now I would think you'd have asked again."

"Asked what?" She felt vaguely irritated to be distracted from this problem with Todd. Before working it out in her head.

"How I found you."

"Oh, that. Did I ask you before?"

Frieda only rolled her eyes, broke the yolk of an egg, and mopped it up with a piece of toast.

"Okay. I'm asking again."

"I was my own private detective. Your father wanted to hire one."

A kind of creeping anxiety in her belly, tangible emotion. "So when you get back, you'll tell him I'm okay. Right?"

"*Are* you okay?"

"Just tell him. Please."

"Right. Like I didn't already call him from my cell phone last night. He's worried about you. We all are. In the state of mind you're in. You know."

"No. I don't know. Tell me."

"You might do something crazy."

"For example."

"Oh, I don't know. Shave your head. Run away from home. Change your name and get a job herding tourists around a state monument. The name thing is weird."

"Why is it weird?"

"Well, not the Annie part so much, being as that's your middle name and all. But the Stewart part. Weird. Very unhealthy. Like you're trying to marry a dead guy or something. Like those nuns that wear wedding rings because Christ is, like, their husband. Very unsettling."

"I've never been compared to a nun before. You still haven't said how you found me."

The waitress appeared with a tall glass of buttermilk. Annie's stomach felt more settled just to look at it. She indicated a spot next to her coffee cup, and the waitress set it there.

"Cook says two dollars." Almost apologetic. "Too much?"

"A bargain at twice the price." She sipped it gingerly as the waitress disappeared again, leaving them alone on the patio. A car full of tourists pulled into the dirt lot, but to Annie's relief they only piled out and took photos, then drove away.

Frieda said, "I just started at Ragged Point. Then next I tried San Simeon. Thought there might be a pattern there."

"And did what in these two places?"

"Just asked about you. Described you. The Big Sur coast is a pretty sparsely populated place. Not as many bald women here as you might think."

"You know why I cut off all my hair."

"Do I?"

"You should."

"Oh. Oh, right. The beauty thing again. You think they only want you for your beauty."

"I know it."

"So is everybody leaving you alone?"

Annie drew on her cigarette and noticed that she wanted to be done with this meeting, to go find Todd and see what damage she'd done. More than anything, noticed a lack of joy at seeing Frieda again. But she didn't know what that meant or how to change it. Merely that it was the case.

Frieda sighed. "I keep trying to tell you."

"Right. I know. Something about spirit."

"Your enthusiasm. Your humor. Your sense of fun."

"You're kidding."

"It must still be in there somewhere, or nobody would be giving you the time of day. It must still show, in spite of the containment unit you've built around it."

"How's Leevon?" Annie said, to have something else to say.

"Fine. I think he misses you. Every time I take him for a walk he tries to drag me down to your house."

"Sure, use your dog to play at my heartstrings. That's fair."

Brief silence. Then Frieda said, "When are you coming home?"

"I'm not."

Long silence. Several minutes, in fact. During which Frieda attacked her breakfast with the enthusiasm she had always shown toward food, killing a good half of it before setting down her fork and looking up again.

Finally, she said, "When I was a kid, my dad was out late one night. Driving a ways out of town and back. It was raining. And I was lying in bed, and I couldn't sleep. And I started thinking. What if he died? He didn't, of course. But if he had . . . Mind you, I was only about six. If he had, I might've thought it was all my doing. Kids are like that. They have this overdeveloped sense of their own power. They think they can make things happen somehow. But we're not kids, Theresa."

Annie put her sunglasses on in the fog. Drew hard once more on the cigarette and crushed it in the glass ashtray.

"I know you mean this to be helpful, Frieda, but it's not."

"What could I do to help, then, Theresa?"

"Well, for one, you could not call me Theresa."

"What's number two?"

"You could go home."

Frieda seemed to sit with that a bit. As if rolling it over somehow. Annie knew that she was hurt but that she wouldn't say so.

"I'm sorry, Frieda. I'm sorry if that sounded hurtful. I realize I'm not being much of a friend right now. But I just can't give you any of what I don't have."

"Fair enough, I guess."

A long silence.

"Did I used to be a good friend?"

"The best. What should I tell your father? And Randy?"

Her first reflex was to say, Tell Randy to go shove it. But it was inappropriate to the moment, she knew. Too much. Too aggressive. It wasn't Randy's fault anyway. It was her fault.

"Tell them I know what I'm doing."

"*Do* you know what you're doing?"

"Probably not. But that's still what I want you to tell them."

When she arrived back home, alone, she decided she did not want to call the guide trailer to ask Todd's last name. Because she hated to bring other people into this. Hated to think of hurting him further by drawing attention to the situation. But otherwise she would simply be sitting home for two days, thinking. Wondering what she had done. So she called.

Zewicki, she was told.

She dug up the phone book, found no listing. Called information, was told there was no Zewicki listed. Then she pulled the phone out of the wall and threw it through her closed living room window. After some time to settle, she picked her way through the potential glass, barefoot, to see out. See if she could locate it. See if it was still retrievable in any way. But as far as she could tell it had rolled down the bank of the mostly dry bed of the Santa Rosa Creek, which abutted her trailer park. And she hadn't the energy to go after it just yet.

She decided to go back to bed, though she doubted she would sleep.

When she woke up it was dark.

She picked her way by moonlight. Through the gap in the chain-link fence. Along the path that bordered beach parking. Across the dry bed of a slough. Onto William Randolph Hearst State Beach. She didn't know the time or care. She hadn't eaten, and she felt hungry, but she also felt—vaguely, without quite putting it into words—that she deserved to be.

She had a blanket around her shoulders, but her scalp was cold. After a couple of months giving tours in ninety-degree temperatures, though, part of her enjoyed being cold. The part of her that thought there was no such thing as cold anymore, that she would never feel it again.

She padded down the beach, hurting her bare feet on rocks and mussel shells, to a spot in front of the old mission-style Hearst warehouse. There she stopped and sat in the sand, which felt cool even through the blanket. Wrapped up every part of herself, pulling the blanket over her head like a hood. And asked James a question she had been meaning—but was afraid—to ask since moving to the neighborhood.

She asked if he was around here anywhere.

While waiting for an answer she may have dozed briefly.

When she woke it was still dark. And no sign that he was there. Even in the most marginal sense. She hoped he

110

was angry with her, upset. Not speaking to her over what—if anything—happened with Todd. Because of the alternative. That perhaps he was nowhere at all.

She found her way back to the car and drove north up Highway 1. Winding around the curves and switchbacks, taking each one a little too fast. Not turning on the heater even though she was cold. Watching for landmarks in the moonlight.

She reached Gorda, which meant she'd been more conservative on the curves than intended. But it also meant she'd overshot her destination. So she found a place to turn around. Hunted more carefully this time. Twenty miles an hour or less.

No Winnebagos on the road at this hour anyway. No other motorists' progress to impede.

When she found the place, she pulled off the road onto the dirt, on the cliff side. Got out and stood looking over the edge. Then sat with her back up against a front tire and hugged herself against the cold and did not go back into the car for the blanket. Watched the intricate pattern of moonlight on water, miles of black water. And thought about the fact that there could be whales out there, lots of them. Just because she didn't see any didn't mean there weren't any out there.

She rubbed her head, feeling the smoothness of fine peach fuzz.

And even though she felt no indications of James, she said a few things to him out loud.

She said, "Nothing I did with Todd was intended as a betrayal of you."

111

And also, "It just came out of being drunk, so whatever it was, even if I just gave him mixed signals, or if something serious happened, it's still something I would never do if I knew I was doing it, so you see it means nothing. Nothing. Whatever it was."

Then, after a suitable silence, "My God, James. What if I hurt him?"

Several minutes later, her voice betraying the shivers, "I think I might not be able to live like this forever."

But James either had no answer or wasn't anywhere near. Or was nowhere at all.

A voice startled her. It said, "Ma'am, I'm sorry to startle you." A real voice.

She looked up to see a man standing by the rear bumper. A little hard to tell in the moonlight but probably a drifter, a vagrant. Because she could see that his hair was long and uncombed and his beard untrimmed. Perhaps she should have been frightened of him, but she wasn't. Something about his soft manner, his polite opening statement.

When she didn't answer, he said, "I just wondered if you were headed south. I was looking to get a ride south, you know? Not many cars at this hour, so I've been walking."

"As soon as I get done here I'm headed back south," she said. Quietly and naturally, as though she'd had many conversations with this man. "I could take you as far as Cambria."

"How far is that from Highway Forty-six?"

"Only about four miles."

"Good," he said. "That's good. I can walk that. That's a real blessing."

He came around the car and sat in the dirt beside her. Neither too close nor too far away. A respectful distance.

She said, "I can drive you on to Highway Forty-six. It's only a few minutes out of my way."

"That would be very nice, if you didn't mind. If you don't mind my asking, who were you talking to just then?"

She looked over at his face in the half dark. Closer now, she could see pockmarks in his skin, a remnant of teenage acne perhaps. He smelled like he hadn't bathed recently, but she felt buoyed by the company and disinclined to judge him. She also knew that many homeless people had mental problems, but she couldn't find the line to separate him from herself even if that were the case.

So she said, "A friend of mine who died."

"Oh," he said. "That's a good thing to do, then."

"Think so?"

"If it helps. When somebody dies, that's such a hard thing. Whatever you do to feel better is a good thing. Do you feel better?"

"Maybe a little bit."

"Well, that's good, then."

"Tell me something. Do you think that when somebody dies he's still around somewhere? Or do you think he just *isn't* anymore? At all?"

The stranger sat with that a moment. Then he said, "I think everybody is somewhere. But as to where somebody is when they've died . . . I'm not smart enough to know that."

113

"No. Me either," she said. "Come on. Let's get on the road now."

They drove down the coast in comfortable silence for a few minutes. She reached into her glove compartment and took out a near-empty pack of cigarettes. Shook one out and took it with her lips and then held the pack out as an offering to her passenger, who'd seemed interested in her movements since the pack appeared.

"That's kind of you," he said. "I could sure use one. But you only have a couple left. Maybe I shouldn't."

"Go ahead," she said. "We can stop on the road and get more."

He took it. Took her offer of a light. Sat back and smoked in satisfaction for a few miles.

"As a matter of fact," she said, "have you eaten?"

"Not since yesterday morning, no."

"Well, we'll stop and get a good breakfast. It's on me."

"You're a kind person," he said.

"No," she said. "I'm not. I wish I could say you're right. I always used to think I was. But it turns out that, when it really counts, I'm not."

"I guess I don't know you," he said. "You seem like a kind person to me."

"Maybe I'm trying to overcompensate."

"Well, whatever the reason, I'll take you up on the of-fer of breakfast."

When the waitress came by, she looked at the two of them, sitting on opposite sides of the booth, and took one step back. Annie and her passenger ordered their break-fasts anyway. She did not take out her pad and write the orders down. When they fell silent again, the three just looked at one another.

Then the waitress said, "Mind if I ask if one of you has money to pay for this?"

Annie reached into her jeans pocket for a wad of bills. Three twenties, a five. A few ones. Laid them on the table in a clump.

"I'm terribly sorry," the waitress said.

"Don't be," Annie told her.

"I really meant no offense."

"None taken."

"What was that second order?" She took her pad out and wrote it all down.

Annie made a mental note to leave her a good tip, to change her expectations for next time, the next cus-tomer.

After the waitress left, Annie looked across the table at her passenger. He looked surprisingly unkempt in this good lighting. "I'd like to ask your advice on something."

He laughed. His teeth were stained but good and straight, and when he laughed he looked like a child. Like the child he must have been at one time.

"What's funny?"

"It's just that nobody's said that to me for a long time. But go ahead."

"Okay. Let's say you have something inside you—a drive, a desire. A force, let's say—that's pushing you to do something that you know in your heart is dangerous. Is it better to resist it? Or would it be better to find an outlet for it? The safest one possible?"

"Well, that depends," he said, blowing on his cup of coffee. Holding it with both hands close to him. Clearly a treasure. "I'd say it depends on whether resisting it is likely to work."

They drank their coffee in silence until the waitress came back with their food.

"Thank you for this," he said before digging in. "This is a great blessing. I'm sorry I wasn't much help with advice."

"No, you were," she said. "You told me just what I needed to know."

She drove him to the corner of Highway 1 and 46 East. Wished him luck. She didn't ask his name because it didn't seem relevant.

FOUR

The Specter Steals Cigarettes

When she arrived home, her phone was back. Sitting on the cinder-block stairs to her front porch. Its cord had been carefully wound around the receiver. Just sitting there waiting for her, like a gift.

When she opened the door and stepped inside, she saw her broken living room window had been carefully covered with a plastic garbage bag. White plastic, taped neatly on all four sides with duct tape. From the outside. She sat down and tried to think. She knew none of her neighbors, and as far as she could tell Frieda had gone home. Todd maybe? He knew where she lived now. Maybe. Maybe Todd.

She tried to reconnect the phone, but she'd pulled the wire out of the little plastic connector, which sat comfortably in the phone jack as if it could fulfill its usual purpose there. She took it out, stared at it, stared at the end of the wire. Wondered whether she could fix it if she had some kind of tool. Pliers, maybe. Those things that people tend to have available in a drawer when they haven't recently run away from home.

Then, feeling too tired to consider it any longer, she went to bed. Tried to catch up on sleep before the morning, when she had to be at work, acting as if nothing had ever been wrong nor ever would be.

She drove in to work an hour early, hoping to get a moment to talk to Todd. It worked out better than she had imagined. As she pulled past the security kiosk, she found him waiting for the next bus up the hill. She pulled over, and he climbed in, as if the whole moment had been carefully arranged.

She said, "I thought you always drove up."

He said, "I thought I did, too. But my truck is making a funny noise. I'm hoping it might last till payday if I leave it at the bottom of the hill."

"About the other night—"

He raised a hand to stop her. "You don't have to say a thing. It's a nonissue. It's all forgotten."

"What's all forgotten?"

His head took on that tilt. "What do you mean?"

"Don't let this get around, okay? But when I drink . . . particularly tequila . . . I've been known to lose big blocks of time. If you know what I mean."

He nodded slowly.

Annie nosed the car around a sharp curve, and a herd of aoudads swept down the brown hill, came to the edge of the road, panicked. She braked, and they crossed in front of the car, leaping and bolting and bumping into one another. Strangely walleyed Barbary sheep with billy-goat beards, descendants of the old Hearst zoo. Still alive and well as a herd after all these years. Maybe fifty of them. Maybe more.

They sat and watched in silence until the last stragglers had crossed. Then she hit the gas again.

Todd said, "Well, anyway. Nothing happened."

"I was worried that I might've given you some mixed signals."

"Not at all. No such thing. We just had a couple of drinks, and then you let me walk you home."

"Thank God," she said, then wondered if he might misinterpret that.

Before she could rephrase the thought, he said, "I tried to call you a couple of times. See if you were okay. But I didn't get any answer."

"I took a drive up the coast. Also, I was having a little trouble with my phone. As you know. Shit. I have a ten-hour day today. Then when I get home I have a guy coming by to fix the window. Not that you didn't do a swell patch on the window."

"I have no idea what you're talking about."

They came around a tight bend and found themselves stuck behind a tour bus. Annie slowed. Said "Shit" again. She wasn't allowed to pass unless the driver indicated she should, a special gesture of permission with his turn signal. "I think that's Wes. He'll never let us by. He lives to torment guides."

"Could be George."

"That would be a major break."

The left rear turn signal on the bus began a welcome flashing, and the bus pulled slightly right. Annie steered around it, waved when she drew level with the driver. Todd waved, too.

"George," she said. "Good old George."

"Good old George started this rumor on the hill that you pulled by him one morning and hiked your skirt up a little. Showed him some leg as you went by. Do you believe that?"

"Yeah, I believe it. But then, I was there."

"You actually did that?"

"I actually did that."

"I can't believe that. We were all so sure he was lying. Why did you do that? No, never mind. That was none of my business."

"He just looked like he needed something like that. You know?"

"Not really. Now I'm jealous. What's this thing you were saying about your phone and your window? I never got what you meant about that."

"Didn't you bring my phone back?"

"No. Where did it go?"

"You didn't tape up my window?"

"No, I wasn't by your house at all. Except when I walked you home."

"Well, that's really weird, then. Because I don't know any of my neighbors. Not even to say hello."

"Maybe one of your neighbors is secretly in love with you."

"Don't even joke about that."

"Oh. Okay. Sorry. I'm always hitting a nerve, aren't I?"

"Not your fault. I'm all nerves." She pulled up to the big iron gate, stopped to run her gate card through the sensor box. A young doe lay in wait by the side of the road. Hesitant. Trying to decide whether to rush through or not. Annie purposely hung back, let her car coast back downhill slightly, and the deer bolted in.

As they drew through the gate, past the guide trailer, Todd said, "You wanted that deer to get in. Didn't you?"

"I like to watch the gardeners all running around like crazy trying to chase them out before they eat the roses. It gives me something to do."

When she arrived home from work it was nearly dusk and the handyman was waiting on her front porch, glancing at his watch. A heavy older man with white hair and a beard, too disagreeable and too intent on watching her body to remind her of Santa Claus. She walked up the cinder-block steps.

"You have to take the window out from the outside anyway," she said, not liking him already. "You could've started."

"Whatever," he said, and went around the back of the trailer.

Annie let herself in, slipped out of her shoes. Sighed, sat down, and began to rub her feet. She wanted to take off her nylons but would have to go into another room to do it. And it seemed like such a long way away.

She took a cigarette from the pocket of her blue polyester blazer. Decided if she ever got smart enough to quit this job she'd never wear polyester again. Which she supposed might have gone without saying, since she'd never once worn it before getting the job. But it felt good to make that commitment all the same.

She lit the cigarette, drew deeply. Closed her eyes and blew smoke toward the ceiling. Set her right foot on her left knee and massaged it again. Opened her eyes to see that disturbing old man staring at her through the broken window. His hands working at the edges of the molding while his eyes worked on her.

She got up and walked out to the front porch, slamming the door. Stood in the cool dusk and drew a second hit and knew she needed to get out of these panty hose.

She set the cigarette in a glass ashtray on the porch rail. Went inside, back to her bedroom, and changed into jeans and a sweater.

Then she walked barefoot back to the front porch to take another hit, but the cigarette was gone. She looked on the porch, thinking it had fallen. Then trotted down the cinder-block stairs and looked in the dirt under the porch rail. It wasn't there. It wasn't anywhere. And there wasn't the slightest breeze. It took her a minute or two to accept that it hadn't fallen. It hadn't blown away. It was gone. It had simply left somehow.

She walked back inside and lit another, too tired to worry about it yet.

The handyman had the old window out, and he was nowhere to be seen, which seemed like an improvement. She walked to the open window space and looked out over the heavily wooded creek bed. Just smoked and looked out. Blew smoke through the missing window and glanced at her watch and wished he'd hurry this up.

Her eyes caught a point of light in the creek bed, a glow. She focused more closely and saw a girl sitting in the greenery, watching her. Staring right back. How old a girl was hard for Annie to say, because the girl was many yards away and partly obscured by brush. And Annie was no good at the age of children anyway, having no siblings and no real reason to care. So the girl could have been as young as eight or as old as thirteen. But she was definitely smoking a cigarette. And her face was dirty, her dark hair shaggy and thin and not recently washed. And she returned Annie's stare flatly. Unafraid. Not hostile exactly, but cool and even. As though the safety of her wild surroundings would support her, provide her with a power she was not about to relinquish to anyone.

The girl lifted the cigarette for another puff, lifted it a bit higher than necessary in front of her face, as if to make a point of it. Brag over the fact that she had it and was far enough away to keep it.

"Yeah, you enjoy the rest of that, you little thief," Annie said, but in a quiet voice not intended to carry.

The handyman returned, and Annie spun away from the window. Grabbed her checkbook.

When she looked up again, all was as it had been. The handyman was staring at her chest, and the creek bed was empty except for the green things. She knew the girl had been there, that she had seen something real, and so wondered why it seemed so dreamlike now. Why she should question whether or not the little thief had ever been there at all.

The following evening, Annie arrived home to see a girl with almost no hair sitting on the stoop outside the trailer next door. Her hair was less than an inch long and badly uneven, as if she'd cut it herself with scissors and no mirror.

Because it took a moment to focus on the girl's face, Annie did not initially notice that she had seen the girl before. The girl returned her stare coolly, which is part of what gave her identity away.

Annie said, "What are you sitting there for?"

The girl said, "I live here."

"You're joking."

"Why would I joke about it?"

"If there was a kid living next door I think I'd know it."

"I'm quiet."

"No shit." She almost apologized for the language, but the girl hadn't seemed surprised, and Annie had to remind herself that a girl this age—eleven or twelve, she decided from this close range—probably knew a few choice words even Annie herself did not.

The girl seemed neither friendly nor hostile, and she was clearly not afraid. In fact, she seemed to absorb the attention, half negative though it was.

Annie said, "What happened to your hair?"

"What happened to yours?"

"I shaved it off."

"Cut mine with a scissors. Mom was pissed."

"I can imagine. Why did you do it?"

"Why'd you do yours?"

"Not sure exactly. Punishing myself, I guess." When the girl didn't answer she added, "Your turn to talk."

"I just thought yours looked cool. Mine's all uneven, though."

"Maybe your mom will fix it up for you."

The girl forced out a sound that could have passed for a snort of laughter. But her face did not change, and no mirth or amusement evolved. "You don't know her. She said it serves me right."

Annie stared a minute more. Nodded. Realized she had nothing more to say. Turned to walk back to her own door. Two steps later it hit her, and she turned back.

The girl's stare had not moved or changed.

"You're the one who brought my phone back. Aren't you?"

"Was that bad?"

"No. It was nice."

"Oh. Then I did."

"How did you know where it was?"

"I was down there. In the creek. I'm down there a lot." When Annie didn't answer straightaway, she said, as if questioned further, "I have to go to the bathroom down there."

"Why? What's wrong with your bathroom?"

"My brother's always in it."

Two kids living right next door. And she hadn't even heard one. "Tell him to get out of there."

"He can't."

"Is he a teenager?"

"He's thirteen."

Annie nodded, thinking that explained it. Wanting not to know more. She felt the wear of her long day. Wanted not to have this conversation.

"Well, you can use mine if you need one."

"Now?"

"Do you need one now?"

"Yeah."

"Okay. Come on."

She opened her front door, swung it wide.

The girl stepped in and looked around. "Saw you got the window fixed."

"How did you even get up that high to patch it?"

"I had to stand on a box."

The two stood awkwardly for a moment, neither speaking, and the girl found her own way to the bathroom. Annie could hear the sound of water, the toilet flush. She sat down heavily and removed her shoes. Lit a cigarette.

The girl came back out and stood with one hand on the door. "Can I have a cigarette before I go?"

"No."

"Why not?"

"They're no good for you."

"They're no good for you, either."

"That's not the point, though. If I smoke, that's called stupid. If I give you one, that's called contributing to the delinquency of a minor. Which you are. I'm still not sure I believe you live next door. I would have heard you."

"I told you. I'm quiet."

"I'd at least have seen you."

"You've seen me. Lots of times. You just never looked. You just never noticed. Not even when I did something nice for you. I had to steal something to get you to notice me."

She swung the door open and slammed it hard behind her.

Annie sat quietly, finished up the cigarette. Then changed into jeans and her most comfortable shoes. Walked down to the market and bought a frozen dinner, a six-pack of Coronas, and two more packs of cigarettes.

Then stopped at the pharmacy on the way home and bought an electric hair trimmer. Not just for the punk, she reminded herself. She'd use it, too. It might even be a step in the right direction. Over a razor, that is.

When she got home, the punk kid was nowhere around. She knocked on the trailer the girl claimed to live in. First nothing, no voice or footsteps.

Then a sudden, panicky, "Who's there?"

"It's just Annie. From next door. Is that you, kid?" Maybe she really did live there.

"Oh. Just a minute." The door swung open. The girl stood with a small, cheap-looking, but all-too-real pistol clutched in both of her hands. Her eyes followed Annie's down to it. "I'll put it away," she said.

"Whose gun?"

"My mom's. We're supposed to take care of this place while she's away."

"You have that thing with her blessing?"

"Well, Barth is supposed to protect us. He's older. But he's in the bathroom."

"Why is Barth always in the bathroom?"

"I guess my mom just wants to know where he is."

Annie furrowed her brow, absorbed that for a moment. Felt tempted to just go home. Avoid the whole mess. But it seemed too unavoidable by now. "Are you telling me he couldn't get out of there if he tried?"

"Well, if he tried hard enough, maybe. But my mom fixed it to lock from the outside. He'd have to break the door or something. She'd kill him."

"Couldn't you just let him out?"

"I used to. But then she came home early one time. Parked out on the street and surprised us. Boy, did I catch it."

"Did she hit you?"

"No. She doesn't usually hit. But she didn't let me come in for two days. It was cold, too."

Annie stepped inside. Gently took the pistol from the girl's hands and set it on the kitchen table, because it made her edgy. Walked down the narrow hallway to the bathroom.

"What's your brother's name again?"

"Barth."

"These trailer bathrooms are so tiny. How long is he supposed to be in there?"

"Well, she usually leaves when we come home from school. Comes home in the morning. She has a boyfriend in Pismo Beach."

"Barth?" No answer. She unhooked the door, a simple hook like the kind you'd use on a screen door. "Barth? It's just your neighbor Annie. I just want to see that you're okay."

She opened the door.

He sat in the bathtub. Holding the sides, as if in a life raft. A skinny teenager with lousy skin but shiny, thick black hair. Clean, too. She supposed he had plenty of chances to wash it. He didn't look the least bit happy to see her. He didn't say anything.

"Would you like to come out of there?"

He shook his head.

"I'll sit right here in your living room. When she gets home I'll tell her I'm the one who let you out."

No reply.

"She'll have to take it out on me."

"Lock the door and go away," he said. His voice seemed high for thirteen. And quiet, as if his lungs didn't hold much air.

"I'm just trying to help."

"Well, you're not helping. You're just going to make it worse. Go home."

Annie blinked a few times and closed the door.

I'll call Child Protective Services, she thought. In the morning. I'll have to. Now that I've seen, I'll have to.

She locked it again with the hook, because he yelled through the door that she should. Annie turned, saw the girl at the end of the hall, watching her. Shook her head, trying to shake away her thoughts, the feeling in her stomach. She pulled the clippers out of the bag.

"Look what I bought."

"What is it?"

"It's for evening up short hair."

"Will you do mine?"

"That's the idea. But let's do it at my house."

Little wisps of black hair fluttered into Annie's sink. Her stomach felt tight and constricted, like she'd just witnessed an accident on the highway.

For a while the hyperactive buzz of the electric clippers provided the only sound.

Then Annie said, "You told me your brother's name but not yours."

"Georgia."

"Georgia. This is looking a lot better, Georgia. I might have to dial it down one more number. Otherwise this little spot will be shorter." She pointed to a spot over and behind the girl's left ear.

"That's fine. It'll be just about the same as yours."

"Pretty damn close. This may sound strange, what I'm about to say. Like it goes without saying. But maybe you don't know. Because maybe you're just used to it. So I'm going to say it. The way your mother treats you guys is not normal. It's abuse."

"I know."

"Did anybody ever try to do anything about it?"

"Yeah. A neighbor once. When we lived in Pismo Beach. But my mom told the police the lady was a liar. And the police said they couldn't prove it."

"So nothing happened."

"Well, it got worse. That's something happening."

"I guess. It's not the something I had in mind."

"Don't," Georgia said.

Annie's eyes came up and met hers in the mirror. The twin haircuts created a strange resemblance, like they must be related by blood.

"Don't what?"

"Call anybody. Barth was right. It'll make it worse."

"I feel like I have to do something."

"Please. Don't."

Annie breathed deeply and let the breath out in a sigh. Turned off the clippers. Without the buzz of them the tiny room echoed with silence.

"I'll think it out real carefully and not do anything right now. How's that?"

Georgia brushed at her head. "I like this," she said. "It looks real good. People will think we're sisters."

She walked out of the bathroom without saying more.

When Annie finished cleaning up the hair, she came out to find that Georgia was gone. So was the open pack of cigarettes she'd left on the kitchen table.

FIVE

Your Children Are the Short Ones

When Annie got home from work the following evening, exhausted in a way that no amount of walking or stair climbing or answering questions could possibly justify, she found Georgia sitting on her front porch.

"Can I sleep at your house?" Georgia said. Before Annie had said so much as hello. When Annie didn't answer fast enough Georgia said, "I got locked out. For smoking."

Annie looked over at the trailer next door. Dark and silent. Too bad, she thought. I'd like to have a word with that woman. "Where's your mother?"

"She left."

"Okay. Come in."

Georgia flopped onto Annie's couch. Picked up the remote control from the coffee table and turned on the TV. The blare of canned laughter fell like an assault on Annie's ruined head.

"Turn that down. Okay?"

Silence. No TV. No answer. She looked to Georgia, who sat quietly staring at her, the cool, steady look missing from her eyes. Annie had never seen her without it.

"I didn't say you had to turn it off. I asked you to please watch it quietly."

"Okay."

The TV sound came back, so muted Annie guessed the girl probably could not follow the dialogue. But she didn't comment.

Just said, "Have you eaten?"

"Not really. I had a peanut butter sandwich for lunch."

"That was lunch. It's almost seven-thirty."

"Well. That's when I ate. Anyway."

"I'll go out and get a pizza."

"Cool."

"What do you like on it?"

"Everything."

"Everything?"

"No onions."

"Okay. Everything except onions."

"No anchovies."

"Got it."

Annie went off into the bedroom and changed out of the rumpled uniform she'd worn and sweated in all day. Changed into shorts and a tank top. Came back out and looked at the phone. Suddenly happy she'd had someone come and fix it.

She ordered a pizza, then sat out on the porch and smoked a cigarette.

Polished off two Coronas and waited for the delivery guy. Because it had dawned on her that it might be better if Georgia were not left alone in her place, with all her things.

In the morning Annie woke before seven to a pounding on her door. She got up, put on a long shirt, and stumbled out into the living room. Georgia was a narrow lump on her couch, the afghan pulled up over her ear.

Annie opened the door.

A plump, bleach-blond woman stood on her porch, looking unhappy. Wearing a short, fancy dress, as if on her way to an evening out. Narrow nose, narrow features. Her eyes narrowed in anger. Clearly Annie had already done something to inconvenience her.

"You been giving cigarettes to my girl?"

Annie stepped outside, though not a hundred percent dressed, and pulled the door closed against her back, thinking it better if the woman never saw Georgia asleep on her couch.

"No," she said. Careful to establish an utter lack of intimidation.

"She said you did. Is she lying? 'Cause if she's lying and she stole them, she's gonna be sorry she was ever born."

"She wasn't lying."

"Well, one of you is."

"I lied. I gave them to her."

"That was a stupid thing to do."

"Of course it was. I'm sorry. I don't know what I was thinking. It won't happen again."

The plump woman took a step closer. Raised her finger to point in Annie's face. "You better not be lying to protect her, either."

Annie took hold of the woman's hand. Forcibly lowered it, then threw it aside. Allowed her emotion, her opinion of the woman, to shine through her eyes suddenly and for the first time. Annie took a step in, though they were standing close already, and the woman backed up a step.

"I must have misunderstood you," Annie said. "I could have sworn you just told me what I . . . had . . . better . . . not . . . do." She allowed a pause, an ominous emphasis, on each word. "Maybe you got me confused with your kids for just a second."

"I just meant—"

"I'm bigger than they are."

"Well. Just don't give her any cigarettes."

"I won't."

"Okay, then. Fine." And the woman hurried away.

Annie wanted to go after her. Or yell after her. Let your goddamned son out of prison. Let your daughter into her own house. You sick, sadistic . . . But it might only make it worse.

So she just stood a moment, feeling that anger turn inward. Trying to reabsorb it. Then she went back inside.

Lit her first cigarette of the morning and started a pot of coffee.

Georgia, who she hadn't known was awake, said, "What did you tell her?"

"I said I gave you the cigarettes but it won't happen again."

"Did she know I was here?"

"I don't think so."

"Good. I better go."

Georgia looked both ways before slipping out the door. Left the afghan lying in a lump on the floor and the impression of her small body in Annie's couch.

It was about ten days later. It was the morning after a long, strange night that Annie had spent in her car outside Todd's house in Cayucos. Carefully not going inside.

When she picked him up at the visitor center and gave him a ride up the hill, she checked him carefully for signs that he knew what she'd done. But there was no reason he would have seen her. And no indication that he had.

Still, she felt she couldn't swim against that tide much longer.

A group of three female trainee guides stood huddled outside the Roman Pool as Annie and Todd made their way down from employee parking. The girls waved too enthusiastically to their tour groups as George transported them off the hill again. George gave Annie a wistful smile as he rounded the circle. The three young women dropped in to walk with Annie and Todd.

One, a dark-haired girl named Mary Lee, said, "Annie, do you think Jeffrey is cute?"

"Yeah. I think he's adorable." Actually, she didn't think much about Jeffrey one way or the other. But she knew it would help him to say that, and there was no reason not to cut a guy a break.

Mary Lee said, "See? I told you so, Margaret."

Margaret said, "A little fat for me."

Annie said, "He's not fat. He's just stocky. It's how he's built. He's big. It's not a crime."

Mary Lee said, "That narrows it down to four, then."

Annie said, "Four what?"

Margaret said, "Mary Lee's in the market for a boyfriend. She kind of likes Jeffrey but also Matt from Housekeeping. And Todd, but don't tell Todd we said that." She said it plenty loud enough that Todd, still walking right along, heard just fine and reddened slightly.

Mary Lee said, "Thanks loads, Margaret."

Annie said, "Who's the fourth?"

"Leander."

"Leander has a girlfriend."

"Not anymore he doesn't. They broke up. Where have you been?"

Annie said, "Well, you know. Give me two days off, you have to retrain me."

At the North Stairs, halfway to the guide trailer, Annie peeled left from the group, up the stairs toward the North Earring Terrace.

The Main Terrace was empty except for Leander. He stood looking right, away from Annie, out over Sekhmet to the Pacific Ocean. The morning was cool, the air livable, and Annie breathed it in and vowed to remember this later in her ten-hour day when the inside of the Big House reached eighty-nine degrees and none of the visitors would stay on the tour mats or keep their oily hands off the choir stalls.

"Leander," she said, and he snapped his head around.

The look on his face changed immediately, as if he'd never meant to be caught having it. Then his eyes reacted to seeing her. In a positive way. In a way they hadn't before, that she could recall. "Annie. Where've you been? I've been wanting to talk to you."

"I heard you broke up with your girlfriend. Are you okay?"

"Yeah. Kind of."

"Taking it well, then."

"Yeah. I guess. No. I'm lying."

"I'm sorry."

"You know, I was just standing here thinking. . . . When somebody you know has a breakup, it never seems like that big a deal. I mean, you know it bites, but it just seems like . . . you know. They'll get over it. It happens to everybody. But then it happens to you. And it's this really big deal. You know?"

"Yeah. I know."

"She was seeing some other guy right under my nose."

"I know."

"I guess everybody did. That's what bites so bad about it. Finally I just said, 'Look, what's it gonna be? I mean, who do you love, him or me?' Know what she said?"

138

"No, but I have a bad feeling I can guess."

"Did you ever have that happen to you? Just suddenly found out the guy you're with would rather be with another girl?"

"Yeah."

"Ever do that to somebody else?"

"Yeah."

"Me too. And I felt bad about it, too. I was real sorry. But now that I know how it feels I'm thinking maybe I wasn't sorry enough."

His eyes left hers, drifted out across Sekhmet again. A heavy bank of dense white fog sat across the horizon, as if drawing his attention. From the side his face looked young, soft, his eyelashes long and dark, like a pretty girl's.

She looked up at the Castle and felt a pang of dread for her ten-hour day. Wondered how she'd get all the way through that. Thought of going home sick. Let them call in a guide who was just dying for more hours anyway. There was a voluntary sign-up list full of them in the supervisor's office. Still, this was summer, and the state hated to send anybody into overtime.

Leander said, "Is it true that you have a crush on me?"

Long pause. Then, "It's more that you remind me of somebody I really cared about."

"Oh. Too bad. All summer I've been really holding on to that. You know? 'Cause all the guys like you, and you don't like any of them, and it made me feel like somebody. That you liked me. All that time while she was making me feel like nobody. Don't think some part of me didn't know what she was doing. There were signs. I guess I didn't want to know."

"I knew you were going to get hurt. I didn't see what I could do to stop it, though."

A long silence, after which she turned to see him looking at her strangely. Curiously. "Well, you weren't supposed to do anything. Why would you even think that?"

Oops. Caught being weird again.

"Long story. I mean, no reason. I mean, I didn't think that. Really. It was just a figure of speech."

When she arrived at the guide trailer, Todd was there, along with what seemed like everyone else on the planet. She tried to catch his eye but could not.

Finally she decided to sit out on the front patio with the older smoker guides instead. And she'd have to smoke fast, too. She had less than three minutes to spare before her Tour Two arrived on the hill.

Five guides sat on the patio. All eyes focused on her as she sat down and lit a cigarette.

"What?" she said.

An older man named Ed said, "Get much sleep last night?"

"You guys need to outgrow this fascination with my personal life. Especially since it's so not fascinating." Had someone seen her?

"We just wanted to hear the inside story on all the excitement."

140

A pang of dread. "Doesn't anybody just live their own life in this town?"

"Well, it's not every day that somebody gets shot in this town. That's a big deal."

Annie sat blinking a second. "Who got shot?"

"Some teenager in that trailer park where you live. You mean you didn't hear anything?"

"Actually, no. I slept like a baby. I do tend to be a heavy sleeper."

Ed said, "My mother was like that. One night this factory down the street exploded, and we were all huddling in the kitchen, like, What was that, what was that? And then—"

"Wait a minute," Annie said. "Wait a minute. I want to know who got shot."

"Some kid shot her brother in the middle of the night. I guess she thought somebody was breaking in. That's all I heard."

The diesel roar of a bus, the metallic sound of the gate drawing open. And it was too late to do anything except conduct a Tour Two.

The minute she put her group on the bus, she retraced her steps to the Main Terrace, but Leander was not there. No Day Security person was there. He could be in the Morning Room, he could be nearly anywhere. But somebody should have been standing under the magnolias.

On her way back to the trailer she spotted him on the Esplanade. Talking to his ex-girlfriend from Gardening. The girl gave Annie a look she found hard to read. She plucked lightly at Leander's shirt and told him she'd see him later, then went back to her job cutting back the purple lantana that spilled over the Esplanade walls.

Annie asked Leander if he could find out about the shooting. "Dispatch would know, right? Wouldn't they know about any sheriff's calls overnight? Maybe you could give them a call. I need to know the names of the kids involved. If it was Georgia. Or Barth."

Leander said, "I'll try to get back to you on that."

She wanted him to say more but he never did.

Twenty minutes later he sent a message down to the guide trailer that the shooter had been an eleven-year-old girl named Cathy Weiss.

Annie breathed again. Chided herself for the foolishness of her assumptions. Then Ed came in and asked her exactly where she had been last night. Said he didn't believe this "heavy sleeper" story.

She was tempted to tell him to shut up but managed to hold her tongue.

When she arrived home that evening, a line of police tape surrounded Georgia's trailer. It filled Annie with a familiar numbness.

A pair of neighbor women she'd never seen, or at least never noticed, stood out front, looking. As though in that absolute void of activity, something significant was just about to occur.

A heavy dusk had fallen, and the moon was already out, hanging nearly full over the dry creek bed. Annie could see a splash of blood on the trailer's stoop. One of the windows was broken. And the more she stood look-ing, the more holes in the trailer's metal shell she noticed. Four that she could see. Quite spread out from one an-other. Like four or five shots had gone wildly wrong. Too bad one had just happened to hit home.

She walked up to the pair of neighbors. Said, "I thought the kid involved with this was somebody named Cathy Weiss."

"That's right," said one of them.

"But the girl who lives here is named Georgia."

"No. The girl who lives here is named Cathy."

"Really? What's her brother's name, do you know?"

"John, I think."

"What happened exactly?"

"Brother was rattling around in the middle of the night and got shot. I guess she thought it was an intruder. Mother's never home, anyway. Poor girl has to fend for herself. Got scared, I guess. Said she thought it couldn't of been her brother because he was in the bathroom. Doesn't make a boatload of sense, but that's what she kept saying. The sheriff took her off for questioning. Got to be an ac-cident, though. Don't you think? Can't see how they can blame a girl her age for a thing like that."

"No, I guess not. I thought her name was Georgia."

The other woman said, "She told me her name was Virginia. And that her brother's name was Montgomery. But I think she just liked to make stuff up."

The first woman said, "Wanted to be somebody better, I guess."

"Did the brother die?"

"Oh yeah. Instantly."

Annie shook her head and walked off.

She let herself into her trailer and sat down hard on the couch.

So Georgia had cut off all her hair, and her name wasn't even Georgia. Just something she picked out to try to be somebody else for a change. That made two coincidences. Two things they had in common.

Annie lit a cigarette and lay down on the couch. Picked up the afghan Georgia had left on the floor so many nights earlier and pulled it over herself. Smoked and looked at the dim ceiling.

Now Georgia had gone and killed somebody.

That's three, she thought.

Then she started to pack.

PART THREE

Journal Entry _____

```
Writing this: Five days after I ran
     away from my new life in San Simeon
Writing about: Right now
```

I have a number of questions. If I had half as many answers, I'd be in great shape.

Question number one: Why did I pick up a pen and start writing in this journal again? I hate this journal. It was never my idea. I only ever did it to make Dr. Grey happy. Okay, let's be really honest here. To keep him off my back. I was never heavily invested in whether or not he was happy. I only picked it up again because I was gathering a few things from my old room. To take over here to Frieda's. I found it under the bed, and I didn't like the idea of leaving it lying around.

But here I am writing in it.

That one is more or less unanswerable. So I'll keep going.

Why did I run like hell all the way back home? If you can loosely call the room over Frieda's barn home.

That one has been running around in my head a lot lately. And I've come up with a number of answers.

I came home to face myself and my situation at long last.

I'm running like a scared rabbit from what happened with that kid.

A weird combination of both of the above.

To even consider the question for very long confuses me.

Then there's the most depressing answer of all. And, unfortunately, the most likely to be true.

I don't know myself well enough to judge.

Moving on. Which, by the way, is becoming a specialty of mine.

I'm going to make a confession to this journal. Since I'm damn well not making any to anybody else. And because somewhere, in some naggy little corner of my mind, I figure this is the reason Dr. Grey got me onto this journal thing in the first place. Like maybe, in some intensely miraculous moment, some weird mood that almost never strikes me, I might tell it something honest.

By the way, that may go to answer question number one. Though potentially true, this is also a stall tactic.

So, marking this day on my calendar.

It goes a little something like this.

The whole leaving-myself-behind thing was a total

crock. Really stupid. Way up there among the stupidest things I've ever done. And God knows it's up there facing a lot of stiff competition.

If I'd thought about it before I did it, I would probably have known this, and then I could have saved myself the trouble. So that's probably why I didn't think it out. Because it was kind of fragile. It would never have held up to the thinking. And I guess part of me knew that, so I left it alone. Let it be delicate and, against odds, weirdly whole.

In hindsight I know more about it than I might have known in advance. If I'd thought it out before doing it, I might have come to a simplistic judgment, like, It'll never work. In hindsight it's a bit more complex.

In hindsight I can see that I left behind my name, my father, my best friend, my home. My hair. All the identity I'd ever had. In other words, everything that was not to blame. And the only thing that *was* to blame I hauled to San Simeon with me.

Ah, logic.

Sudden insight: Is it possible that I've just answered all my own questions?

No. After reading back, I guess not all of them. That one about whether I came back to face things or evade them. That one I've left hanging.

Or, more realistically, I guess it's hanging me.

Journal Entry _____

Writing this: Six days after I ran away
        from my new life in San Simeon
Writing about: My first day back

I realize I haven't said all that much about my father. Anybody who knows my father will realize that it's because there's very little to say.

After the whole "incident," he just sort of disappeared. He had that new girlfriend. I don't even know if they're still together. I didn't ask. Thing about my father is, he doesn't like problems. Not that anybody does. But he absolutely refuses to acknowledge that they exist. So he has to spend a lot of his life getting out of the way.

I guess that might answer some questions about where I got that from.

He paid for my therapy. That was his way of dealing with the crisis. If I had a paid professional to talk to, I was set. I didn't have to, God forbid, discuss anything with him. Then he went to his girlfriend's a lot, and that was pretty much that.

On the day I packed my things and moved out, he wasn't even home.

Enough said about that, I guess.

So about four months later, there I was standing on his welcome mat. The front stoop of the house I grew up in. I knocked on the door. Amazingly, he answered. He was home. Or maybe it's not so amazing. Maybe he was always home. Just as soon as I wasn't.

He looked at me for a split second before it hit him. Who I was.

That surprised me. That caught me off guard, I had to admit.

I have no idea how much I have or have not changed. I didn't spend those four months up the coast seeking out mirrors. I assume most of the change is on the inside, but I guess those things have a way of seeping through the cracks. I'm not trying to exaggerate here. I mean, it was less than a second. Just a beat in the huge continuum of time. But it showed me something. Whether it's something I wanted to see or not is hard to say.

Then he said, "Oh."

I waited. There had to be more than just "Oh."

A painful silence, in which I realized that my very presence on his mat constituted a nasty trauma. And he had nowhere to run.

Finally I said, "I just wanted you to know I was okay."

"Oh," he said again. He looked tired. More than four months older. Or maybe those were just the eyes through which I was viewing him. "Well, Frieda told me you were okay."

Another painful silence. During which I was still not exactly invited in.

Then he said, "Are you back, then?"

I could tell he was trying very hard to sound like that was not a bad thing. But it was. To him, it was.

I'm not stupid. I'm also not overly inclined to take a thing like that personally. My father loves me. This goes without saying. If I were happy and without problems, he'd be more than willing to coexist with me. But of course I was no such thing.

I said, "I thought I'd stay over at Frieda's." His brow furrowed slightly. Probably at the thought of Frieda's parents and their famously reckless habits. "She has that empty room over the barn," I said. Her parents never bother to venture into that great outback, I didn't say. "I thought it might be a good place to . . ." The honest ending to that sentence would have been the word "hide." ". . . get myself together. For a while."

"Oh." That was his favorite word on the day I returned from self-imposed exile. "Okay. Yeah. Good."

Another painful silence. I guess neither one of us wanted to address my exact reason for knocking on his door. Something struck me suddenly, but it's hard to put into words. Some understanding of the world. Why it's in the shambles it's so often in. If this is what we call family.

"I just came to get a few more of my things. From my room."

"Right. Of course." He said it quite brightly. His relief shone through the cracks between each word.

I gathered up some more clothes. My old teddy bear that I've had since childhood. This journal from under the bed, which I only just remembered at the last minute.

Frieda wasn't home, but I went up to the room over the barn anyway. Set down my things but didn't unpack. It seemed wrong to unpack without permission. Even though I knew Frieda would never refuse me the room.

Leevon escorted me up and stayed with me. He's a host of a dog, Leevon. The sort of dog who will practically pour you a drink as you walk in the door.

I asked him if he had a cigarette, but he only looked at me curiously. It seemed to make him nervous when I asked him something he didn't understand. So I dropped it altogether. Though I hadn't had a cigarette for a couple of days and was just about to jump out of my skin.

I lay on the bed and cried for the first time in as long as I could remember. Leevon worried about me. He kept bumping my ear with his cold nose.

He's better at many things than my father. Or, for that matter, me.

ONE

Still More Questions

I think I'd been in the room over the barn detoxing cold turkey off cigarettes for a couple of days when I heard a knock at the door.

Leevon barked. Which alarmed me. Because that meant it wasn't Frieda. Then again, I knew it wasn't Frieda, because she would have just opened the door and come in. But it was more the bark that alarmed me. If Leevon was scared, so was I. My heart rate jumped wildly.

I didn't answer it straight off. Leevon growled low in his throat while I ran a quick mental list of who even knew I was up here. My father. It could be my father. But that would mean he was voluntarily walking in the direction of trouble, which seemed unlikely. Frieda would never have told her parents I was here. But maybe they found out somehow and had come to evict me. Seemed like something that involved too much gumption for either one of them. But people have their moods. You never know.

Another knock. Leevon let out one stiff howl. It struck me that he wouldn't bark at Frieda's parents, either. He has a sense of smell. All dogs do.

"Who is it?" I called. Sounding every bit as paranoid as I felt.

"Annie?" A kid's voice. Almost like . . . *the* kid. Not just *a* kid. But of course that was impossible.

"There's no one by that name here," I said through the door. Feeling foolishly satisfied and righteous about the truthfulness of that statement. I had admitted to myself, one member of the family, and one good friend that my name was, in fact, Theresa.

"Her car is out front. Do you know where she is?"

It was the kid.

Or an auditory hallucination. Quitting smoking cold turkey was making me feel weirdly emotional and disconnected from reality. Maybe I was having a sort of waking nightmare.

Against my better judgment, I opened the door.

"It *is* you," she said. "I thought it sounded like you."

Her hair was still only about an inch long, and she was filthy. Her clothes were dirty, her face was dirty. Her hands looked grimy. She looked something like I felt.

I was beginning to gather that I was not imagining this. Though I hated to let go of such a welcome theory.

"What are you doing here?"

"Can I have a cigarette?"

"What are you doing here?"

"Just one. I haven't had one for days."

"How did you find me here?"

"It wasn't hard." She scratched her nose. Looked once at my face. But I guess she didn't like what she saw there, because she looked down at the doormat immediately. "Your mail was forwarded from here."

"So you looked in my mailbox."

"Yeah. Sorry. I know your name is really Theresa. Your checks from the Castle came to Theresa, too. I guess you had to tell them your real name, huh?"

"And I know your name is really Cathy. What are you doing here?"

"Please can I have a cigarette?"

"I don't have one. Wait. My mail was forwarded from home. Not from here."

"Right. That man at your house told me you were here. Is that your father? What do you mean you don't have one?"

"I quit, okay? What are you doing here?"

"Can I come in? Hey, cool dog. Is that your dog?" Leevon was poking his nose through the partly opened door, licking in the general direction of the kid. Leevon liked kids.

It struck me that the conversation was spinning like a dog chasing its own tail. I was getting nowhere. Maybe it was the nicotine deprivation, but the whole thing was making me feel irritated. Actually, it was probably irritating enough all on its own.

"I've asked you about six times what you're doing

here. I'm not letting you in unless you answer my question." The minute it was out of my mouth I realized I'd bargained off too much too cheaply. Now if she answered, she could claim I'd said I would let her in.

She looked down at the mat again. "My mom threw me out. For good this time. I got nowhere else to go."

More nicotine-withdrawal-related outrage. "She can't do that."

"Wanna bet?"

"You're eleven. She can't just put you out on the street."

"You wanna go tell her?"

I sighed. And with the sigh, all the irritation and outrage drained away and was immediately replaced by surrender and depression. I didn't have the strength to fight anything that was so inherently bad. "How did you get here?"

"Took a bus to San Luis Obispo. That was all the money I had. Stole that out of her change jar the day before she kicked me out. Had a feeling it was coming. Hitchhiked the rest of the way."

I sighed again. "What kind of person picks up an eleven-year-old girl and doesn't even ask what she's doing away from home? You could have been killed."

We both squirmed a bit at my admission that I cared, on some level, whether she lived or died.

"Do-gooders," she said. "I told them your house was home. That I was lost and they were taking me home. People are stupid. They'll believe anything."

And you'll tell any lie, I thought. And I'm not that stupid.

But I opened the door. So maybe I am.

Leevon poured her a drink.

Hard to say how long I sat there on the bed with her, watching her bite her nails. Could have been thirty minutes. Could have been three minutes that felt like ten each.

I wanted to tell her to cut it out. The nail thing. Because it was making me nervous. But I'd been plenty nervous before she showed up. So that didn't seem fair.

Finally I said it. Because it needed saying. Even though it went without saying. I guess you had to be there. It made sense to me.

I said, "You know you can't stay here. Right?"

She shot me this wounded look. Just for a split second. Then she armored over it, trying to look bored and cool and a little bit angry. My stomach dropped into my shoes. She hadn't known that. I really would have thought she'd known.

"Why can't I?"

"Oh my God," I said. I honestly didn't know where to start. "Look around you. What do you see?"

She looked around. A bit defensive. Or detached. Like I had asked her to do some bothersome homework. And she was more or less just phoning it in. "A nice place. It's cool."

"One room. With one tiny bathroom. No kitchen. No refrigerator. One twin bed."

"I'll sleep on the floor."

"No kitchen," I repeated.

"We'll eat out."

"And I assume you'll be picking up the check?"

I regretted that. As soon as I said it. It was a valid truth. But the delivery felt harsh.

More valid truth. I was getting low on money myself. I needed to get a job. I'd been eating fast food and allowing Frieda to sneak me leftovers. I honestly couldn't afford anyone else on the tab.

But oh my God. That was so only the beginning.

"Look," I said. "This place is barely a home for one. I'm sorry."

"That's not why," she said. "That's not really the reason. You just don't want me."

"Kid," I said. The name thing still had me slightly off balance. "I don't even want *me*."

"That doesn't make any sense." She had stopped biting her nails. Switched to hugging and kissing Leevon. Not realizing that her vulnerability was showing.

"What I mean is, just taking care of myself . . . just turning my own mess back into a life . . . I'm not even sure I'm up to doing my own stuff right now."

"I won't be any trouble. I promise. I'll help. I'll clean up. I'll find some ways to make money or something."

"You can't stay here," I said. With a finality that sounded really sad. Even to me. "I'm sorry."

Silence hung for quite a long time. Then I reached out to put a hand on her shoulder. Not hard to do. That little room was so small that two people couldn't really get far outside touching distance. She jerked away. Jumped to her feet. I had let the cork out of the bottle. She was pissed.

"I'm not going into foster care! I'm not! My friend Tara was in foster care. I'll live on the street before I let them get me. I'll run away."

"Down, girl," I said. "You already ran away." She sat on the bed again, looking more than a little defeated. "Now let's just calmly consider our options here. What do you have in the way of blood family?"

She was looking down as I asked the question. Down and partly away. She sniffled quietly. Wiped her nose on her sleeve. That's when I got that she was crying. But not for effect. She was trying hard to hide it. "Not much. Just a grandmother in Bellingham. But she won't take me."

"Where's Bellingham?"

"Washington State. Way up near Canada. It's pretty there. We were up there once. But she won't take me."

"How do you know?"

"She's Harold's mother. My dad. He died. I called him Harold. She hates my mother."

"You're not your mother."

"Close enough, though."

"We could call her."

"She doesn't have a phone."

"You're joking."

"Not so much, no."

"Who doesn't have a phone in this day and age?"

"My grandmother. For one."

As I stopped to try to imagine such a thing, it struck

me that I was taking the word of what you might call an unreliable narrator. In other words, a liar.

"Are you lying to me so I won't call her?"

She raised her hand as if in a court of law. "May God strike me dead if I'm not telling the truth."

She didn't glance up at the sky or anything, as if expecting a lightning bolt. Not exactly ironclad proof. But I figured there was maybe a sixty or seventy percent chance that her grandmother honestly didn't have a phone.

"I don't know what we're supposed to do here," I said. I didn't realize how defeated I felt until I heard myself say it.

"Me neither," she said.

I mean, I couldn't just put her out on the street. Could I? I resented having somehow become responsible. I tried to track how and when that had happened. But somehow it had happened. If I put her out, she might end up dead. And someone could come to me and say, You *what?* You put a defenseless eleven-year-old girl out on the street by herself? Why didn't you help her?

No one *would* come to me and say that, of course. I would do it to myself.

I said, "I guess you'll have to stay here just until we figure out what to do with you."

"I'm not going into foster care," she said again.

"Yeah, I got that."

"If I find out you called Child Protective Services, I'm gone forever."

"Oh, now there's a threat that has me shaking in my boots."

That seemed to bump her out of her gangster mode and remind her she was a lost child with precious few options.

I chewed on our precious few options for a few moments. Until she said, "What are you thinking about?" Like whatever it was, I could hurt her just by thinking it.

"I was wondering if my piece-of-crap old car would make it almost as far as Canada."

A long silence. I could hear her breathing. I could feel the world—at least her world—freeze solid into her fear.

"What if she won't take me?"

"I think it might be harder to say no if she was looking you right in the face."

"But what if she won't?"

Good question, actually. But when only one possible option remains, I find it best not to question it too thoroughly. And I said so.

After that she didn't have much to say. So I guess the doubts were more or less all she had.

Journal Entry _____

```
Writing: The day the kid showed up
About: Now
```

To fail to see the significance of this thing, a person would have to be blind, deaf, dead, and stupid. Maybe I flatter myself, but I like to think I'm none of the above.

It's as plain as the nose on my face. The Universe has sentenced me to perform community service.

It's about time someone sentenced me to something. Someone besides me, that is. Which is not to say I'm the least bit happy about it.

First of all, I've had to slip down into the barn just to get the privacy to write this. And the barn is the last place I saw James alive. So that's not fun at all.

Second of all, how am I supposed to help somebody get through something when I'm completely lost in that same something myself?

Journal Entry _____

Writing: The night of the day the
    kid showed up
About: Now

Last-minute change of plans. The kid is sleeping up in my little room. With Leevon. I'm down in the barn.

It's sort of hard to explain.

I couldn't sleep in the same room with her. The room is just too small. And she kept looking at me. I was getting claustrophobic.

It's not so bad down here. I know I just complained about it last time I wrote in this journal. I haven't forgotten that. But I was just weirded out by the whole James thing. It's not exactly like the whole "barn as it relates to James" thing has evaporated. It's more like it's stopped feeling so bad to me. It almost feels like a good thing.

I can remember his face tonight. Not struggle to put it together feature by feature. Remember it. Not just the

164

hair color and the shape of his face but fully animated, actual James. I can picture him over in the corner of the barn, getting me a soda.

Just in my imagination. I'm not hallucinating.

I miss James.

But that's not really fair, in a weird way. Because if he'd just walked out of my life that night, I'm not sure I ever would have. It's genuine, my missing him. But why did it take a thing like that to wake it up?

Something about the whole thing doesn't seem right.

The coolers are gone from the corner of the barn. Of course. The only leftover from the party is the hay and the straw. I guess there was no point dragging out all that hay and straw.

So I'm fairly comfortable in the stall where James and I . . . were.

It seemed wrong to kick the kid downstairs. Make her sleep in the barn. Like child abuse or something. She's been evicted plenty enough for one lifetime.

And I'm really okay down here.

I wonder if I'll feel better after I've done my community service. I wonder, also, if just giving her a lift to Bellingham will turn out to be enough. Maybe I'm also supposed to know how to help her deal with what happened. In which case I'm going to have to learn whatever it is I need to know as I go along.

I figure we'll leave tomorrow. So I guess I'm going to have to find wisdom tonight in my sleep.

TWO

Betrayals Large and Small

So that's what I get for allowing about a cubic millimeter of soft spot to form in my heart for that juvenile delinquent. I gave her my bed and slept in the barn, and this was how she repaid me. I got home in the morning with this pathetic bag of fast-food breakfast for both of us, and the little shit was lying on the bed reading my journal.

The minute she saw me, she threw it back under the bed.

"Ah," I said. "Very good. Now it's all erased again. Now you've rewound time and nothing is wrong at all."

I was still in the process of processing my anger. And we both knew it.

She sat very still with her eyes wide, waiting for me to say it.

So I did. "Get out."

A long silence. No movement. No glorious lack of juvenile delinquent journal invader.

Then she said, "Out?"

"That would be the operative word, yes. Out."

"You mean, like, for good?"

"Yes. It will be very good to have you out."

"But you were going to drive me to my grandmother's."

"Yes. I was. Before you betrayed my trust completely."

She slunk out without further comment. I was beginning to see her mother in a slightly new light. There was definitely something about the kid that made you want to see her walk out the door.

Sometime around dark the door opened and Frieda walked in without knocking. See? I'm occasionally right about something.

She had a pile of my clean laundry in her hands. Stuff I had left in the dryer. She had even folded it. Frieda is like that.

"Okay," she said. "Tell me the story about the kid sitting on the curb."

For reasons hard to explain, I decided not to hit that one head-on. "Now why would you even notice a kid sitting on a curb? What's it to you?"

"It's making my parents paranoid. Or I guess I should say *even more* paranoid. They're hiding behind the curtain, drinking vodka and peeking out the window at her. They probably think she's some kind of miniature CIA agent watching the house."

167

She might have been exaggerating to be funny. But with her parents you never know.

"So why would you think I know the kid-sitting-on-the-curb story?"

She pulled a very small pair of jeans off the top of the pile. Much smaller than I could ever wear. They were, in fact, the kid's jeans. "Maybe because she's sitting out there in hugely oversized jeans and a T-shirt I know is yours, and some clothes her size seem to have made it into your load of laundry. That and the fact that you and the little curb sitter are just about the only two females in the world with that rather unusual haircut."

I rubbed my eyes. Sighed. "Do I really have to tell you the story? Or can I just go out and take care of it?"

"You're not much of a storyteller," she said. "I'll take door number two."

The kid glanced over as I sat next to her on the curb. But she said nothing. We both said nothing. For a truly bizarre length of time.

Then she said, "I wanted to know something about you. You don't tell me anything. I wanted to know the things you won't tell me."

"The things I won't tell you are none of your business."

"I'm sorry."

"It's not that easy. You can't just do bad shit and then say you're sorry. Two words don't erase what you did." A long silence fell as I considered my words in light of what she might have just read in my journal. Speaking of the

168

things we do wrong. But maybe she had only read a couple of pages. Which was probably still enough. "How much did you read?"

Long pause. "Up to the part where you were talking to your father. After you came home."

"So basically just about all of it."

"I guess." Long pause. "I'm sorry."

"Yeah, you said that."

"Except I'm not. I mean, I am. But if I hadn't, I wouldn't have known . . . you know."

I raised a finger and pointed it at her nose in warning. But it took me a minute to figure out how the warning was going to go. "Don't start thinking I have what you need. Because I don't. Don't think I can march you through what to do after something like this happens, because I'm still totally lost in it myself. If I can't even save myself, how am I supposed to save you? It's pretty hopeless, kid."

She chewed on that a moment. Then she said, "At least we're in trouble together." A bit too brightly, I thought.

"God. What did I do to deserve you? Oh. Never mind. I just remembered."

We sat quietly for a minute longer. I could hear crickets singing, and a tree frog. They have big lungs, those tiny frogs. A guy rode by on a bicycle with flashing reflector lights blinking in the dark. I envied him. I wanted his life. I knew it was simpler than either of ours. Probably better than the lives of two pathetic curb sitters put together.

I said, "I ate both of our breakfasts. Hours ago. But I

might have an energy bar or something. You get to sleep in the barn tonight. We'll leave in the morning."

"So you're still gonna take me?"

"I have to do *something* with you."

"Thanks. I really am sorry about the journal."

"Let's just try to get some sleep. We've got a long trip ahead."

Journal Entry _____

The last entry I will ever write in
    this journal

I really only took it out because I was going to destroy it. Seriously. I was going to rip out all the pages a few at a time and burn them in the bathroom sink. But I couldn't bring myself to do it. Some weird little thing in the back of my head says I wrote it all down for a reason and I might want to see it all laid out. Someday.

Besides, now that I've quit smoking, I don't have a match. I don't have one single item designed to create fire.

I like to think the first reason is more important.

On the other hand, I'm damn sure not putting any more of my guts out in black and white so other people can sneak a look without my permission.

I think when I'm done with this final entry I'll fold this journal up in a sweater and put it in the drawer.

Hopefully it will be safe while we're gone. After all, the little sneak thief will be with me.

Speaking of the devil, as I write this she's using my laptop. Visions of hard-drive crashes dance in my head. But she swears she just wants to look up directions to her grandmother's house. But I might be getting better at knowing when she's lying. And she might have been lying. But I'm not sure. Maybe I'm being too suspicious. Hard to blame me by now.

I only get a wireless connection about half the time. And I have no printer up here, so she has to write down the directions. Which may explain why she's taking so long.

Meanwhile I'm trying not to obsess about her teeth.

She came here with the clothes on her back. Which means no toothbrush. Which means it's been about three days since she brushed her teeth. And we'll be another two or three days on the road.

I guess we have stops in our future.

What a note to end on, eh? Somebody else's teeth. But this is the end. My journaling days are over. Not a moment too soon.

THREE

Irritating Role Reversals

So there we were. Headed up Highway 101 in my crappy old car. With the juvenile delinquent journal invader sneak thief in the shotgun seat. We hadn't made any stops yet. I was trying not to obsess about her teeth. No point being codependent. After all, they were her teeth. Not mine.

Things were actually looking fairly good. Something about the aimless, unfinished feeling of driving. I'm loath to admit it, but I actually had that Willie Nelson song, the one about being on the road again, running around in my brain.

It might almost have been a good day.

Then the kid opened her mouth.

"So we have to go through San Francisco anyway. Right?"

I glanced over at her. Sensing a bit of subtext.

"Not exactly. Why?"

"Doesn't this road go to San Francisco?"

"Yeah. More or less. But we're going to skirt around it. Not go right through the city. Otherwise we'll get bogged down in traffic."

"Oh." Disappointment. Subtext.

A knotty feeling in the pit of my stomach. Which means I'm smart enough to know when I'm about to be sucker punched.

"Why? What's in San Francisco?"

"Nothing."

"Then why are you asking?"

"No reason. I guess."

I sighed. "Why not just spit it out, kid?"

"If we're not going through there, then it doesn't matter."

"Okay. Theoretically. Let's just say for the sake of conversation that we were about to go through San Francisco. What's in San Francisco?"

"I just thought maybe we could stop and see James's mom."

My foot hit the brake with no forethought whatsoever. And stayed there. The driver behind me leaned on his horn and then passed me on the left. I pulled over onto the shoulder. Pulled on the hand brake. I could feel my heart racing. I could hear my pulse pound in my ears. Feel it throb in my neck. I held the wheel tightly so I would never need to know if my hands were shaking. But I suspected they might be.

We sat there for a moment in this overpowering silence.

"Would you please repeat what you just said to me?"

She started to open her mouth, but I cut her off at the pass.

"No. Stop. Don't say it. Don't ever say that collection of words in that order ever again."

More silence. She was looking down at her lap.

"How do you know James has a mother in San Francisco? *I* didn't even know that, and I knew James."

"It wasn't hard."

"But *I* didn't even know it."

"You could have. If you'd wanted to."

She pulled a folded sheet of paper from the back pocket of her jeans. More than a little bit dog-eared. Handed it over to me.

Now I would have to loosen my death grip on the wheel, answering the question about my hands. Just as I suspected, they were a little shaky.

I unfolded the paper.

In loopy, surprisingly legible handwriting, the kid had written, "He is survived by his father, James Stewart, Sr., of Reno, Nevada, and by his mother, Lorraine Bordatello, of San Francisco."

"You found his obituary."

"Yeah."

"Did it say anything about brothers or sisters?"

"No, just a mom and dad."

"Great. Nice to know it was their only child I killed. So you found this on the Web at the same time as you were getting directions to your grandmother's."

"Oh. I forgot that."

"You never got directions to your grandmother's?"

"Sorry. I got excited that James's mom lived on our way. And I forgot."

"Then how are we supposed to find your grandmother? Do you at least have her address?"

"Yeah. I know it by heart. We can get a map or stop for directions or something when we get to Bellingham."

I handed her back the paper and she folded it up again and stuck it back in her pocket.

I watched my side mirror for a gap in traffic and then pulled onto the highway with a slight screech of tires. Trying to head north calmly. As if nothing had ever happened.

"Are you mad at me?" she asked a mile or two later.

"Oh, no more so than usual."

"So are we going to stop and see James's mom?"

"No."

"Oh."

About ten miles of silence. That I was hoping would last.

"Why not?"

"Why would I want to see James's mother? She's just about the last person in the world I want to see."

"You could confess."

"Ah. Now it sounds much more appealing."

"It might help."

"And when she screams at me and cries and says I murdered her only son? Tell me how this is going to help?"

"Because you can just look her in the face and say, Well, anyway, I came and told you the truth and that's the

176

best I can do. And then you'll always know. That you did the best you could do."

"Let's not talk for a while."

"Okay."

We drove in blessed silence. We didn't even talk when we stopped at a supermarket and bought a toothbrush and toothpaste, and trail mix for lunch and dinner.

I was attempting to wrap my brain around the sudden change in logistics. I'd just become marginally comfortable with the idea that I would somehow lead the kid out of her guilt and trauma. Even though I knew I didn't know what I would need to know to lead anybody out of anything. But I thought it would dawn on me. I thought I'd get a brainstorm and pass it on. I fully expected to step up to the role of leader.

The idea that the kid knew more than I did about the subject was just plain irritating.

Turned out the juvenile delinquent came with a small consolation prize. A moving car tended to put her to sleep. Even in broad daylight.

It was just barely dark when I found us a Motel 6 in either Berkeley or Oakland, I'm not exactly sure which. I let her sleep while I paid for the room, running up a credit card bill I'd need a job to pay off.

Back when I had a mother, my mother told me that Motel 6 got its name because a room used to cost six bucks. I suppose it would be inconvenient for them to change their name now to Motel 46.95. But part of me felt like they owed it to me to try.

177

I had to actually go back to the car and poke her in the ribs to let her know we'd gotten somewhere.

"What?" she said. She had a bit of dried drool at the corner of her mouth.

"We're stopping."

"Where are we?"

"The East Bay."

"What's an east bay?"

"It's a place."

"But where is it?"

"On the east end of the bay. Hence the expression."

"What bay?"

"The San Francisco Bay." I'd been trying so hard not to say it. "Now will you please come in? I need to get some sleep before I go on."

I opened the door to our tiny, cheap second-floor room. As promised, it had two beds. Besides that, I really didn't care.

The kid flopped onto a bed immediately.

"Brush your teeth," I said.

"Oh. Right."

While she was gone I got undressed. Put on just a long T-shirt, from my little overnight bag, as pajamas. I don't generally use pajamas, so I'd had to improvise. I pulled another clean T-shirt out of my bag and threw it on the kid's bed.

Then I got under the covers. I wanted this night to be over before any more questions could happen.

She came out and stood over her bed. "Is this for me?" she asked, holding up the T-shirt.

"Yes."

"Thanks."

"You're welcome."

"So are we going to see Lorraine Bordello?"

That was just the question I'd been trying to avoid. I wanted to be pissed but ended up laughing at her mispronunciation instead. Just a little snort. I was tired and not filtering my reactions well.

"What's funny?"

"It's Bor-da-tell-o."

"So? I was close."

"Not really, kid. A bordello is . . . like a brothel."

"What's a brothel?"

"It's like a bordello. Will you please stop asking so many questions and go to sleep?"

"Okay, okay. So in the morning we're just driving on again?"

"I'll figure that out in the morning. Now go to sleep."

The good news is, she did. Almost immediately. The bad news is that, when sleeping on her back in an actual bed, the kid snored like a buzz saw.

FOUR

Grace

I woke up to find the juvenile delinquent sitting on the edge of her bed, fully dressed. Staring at me. She said, "It's about time you woke up. It's after eleven."

"Well, excuse me. I didn't get to sleep most of the way up in the car like you did. I also lay awake half the night listening to you snore."

"I do *not* snore."

"How would you know? You're always asleep when it happens."

"So where are we going today?"

"Grace Cathedral."

"No, seriously."

"I'm serious. Grace Cathedral."

"How did that even get on the list? I thought it was either go to Bellingham or go see James's mother."

"I added a third option."

"A church?"

"Not just any church. Grace Cathedral."

"What's so special about it?"

Truthfully, a great deal that I was not prepared to explain. But I had been going over it in my head during the many sleepless parts of the night.

The first—and, coincidentally, only—letter I got from my mother after she left was postmarked San Francisco. It had two photos in it from Grace Cathedral: one of the rosette-shaped stained-glass window in front, another of the labyrinth on the floor inside. She said she had taken off her shoes and walked the labyrinth slowly in her socks, like a meditation, and it had changed her whole perspective. Awakened something in her. I don't remember much more than that, detail-wise, but I could read between the lines. It was a huge and fascinating and beautiful world, especially compared to the one she'd left behind. Someday I'd see that and I'd understand. Maybe even forgive her.

I think she ran off with another man, but it's just a theory.

"It has a labyrinth."

"I don't know what that is."

"Like a maze. Only you can't get lost in it because it doesn't have sides. It's just like a maze on the floor. Like a rug that has this complicated path woven into it. You walk this complicated, twisty path to get to the center."

"So you have to, like, pick the right path? Like a lab rat or something?"

"No. There's just one path. It just winds around and it always leads you to the center."

"And then what?"

"Then you walk out again."

A predictable silence. Yes, we were becoming predictable.

"Why?"

"It's like a meditation."

"Sounds incredibly boring."

"Yes. Well, be that as it may," I said, "that's where we're going."

"Is it in San Francisco?"

"Yes."

"While we're there . . ."

"Do *not* finish that sentence. Go brush your teeth."

"I just brushed them last night!"

"Wow. Your dentist would be so proud. If you had one. Go brush them again."

Parking in San Francisco is a challenge. To put it rather simply. We drove around block after block waiting for somebody to pull out. Unfortunately, by the time somebody did, we'd managed to get ourselves about eleven blocks from Grace Cathedral.

So we walked.

"That's a big church," she said when it came into view. "I don't think I want to go inside. I don't believe in God."

"I didn't ask if you believe in God. For that matter, I didn't ask you to come in."

We climbed the stone steps together. The closer we got to the church, the slower she climbed. She was acting like churches bite. "Do *you* believe in God?" she asked.

"Um. Probably not the same way as the people who built this church did."

"Are you trying to decide about James's mother? Is that why you're going in?"

"No. I'm going in to walk the labyrinth."

"But you're trying to decide?"

"I'm trying to avoid answering questions about it."

"I thought maybe you figured God would tell you if you had to do it or not."

"No. I don't figure that. I figure I have to figure it out for myself. Are you coming in or not? You scared of a little old church?"

"It's a *big* church. And I don't believe in God."

"Then it can't possibly hurt you to come inside."

I held the door open for her. She followed me in. But she looked a little spooked. So maybe she believed in God just a little bit.

The church floor was cool, a cool I could feel right through my socks. And solid. Well, of course it was solid. I realize that sounds pretty basic. But it was an almost exaggerated solid. Like a message to ignore what was in my mind, because what was under my feet was real.

Then I looked up. And you know what? The kid was right. It was a *big* church. For a split second I understood why she was so intimidated. There was something about the place that drew your eyes up. The sheer height of it. The massive stone pillars. The several-stories-tall windows that looked like elongated tablets for the Ten Commandments. The sheer size of the indoor space it created gave it a weight, an importance. And some authority over me. Light shone through the many stained-glass windows and made me feel unimportant and small.

I walked the labyrinth slowly. I think you're supposed to walk it slowly. It was supposed to be a meditation. Right? So I had to go slow and think what I was doing.

Except I really wasn't thinking at all.

I looked up at the rose window once. It didn't have my answers. I saw my mother's face once in my head. Which is interesting. Because I haven't seen her in so long. I usually can't remember it that well. She had no answers for me, either.

When I got to the center an eternity later, I looked up to see the kid staring at me. She looked curious more than anything else. Hopeful. Like she couldn't imagine how this could help, yet she was willing to believe it could.

That's when I realized I had to have an answer. By the time I retraced my path out of there, I would have to know. But I still had very few thoughts during the trip out.

When I saw I was running out of labyrinth, I got in touch with my fear. It came up from my gut and froze me all over. I was terrified of James's mother. It was just suddenly there. Which is amazing. Because most of the time I have no idea what I feel.

Just like that, I had my answer: it didn't matter if I was

afraid. If it was the right thing to do, I had to do it. Fear or no fear. My fear was irrelevant. It did not exempt me. It was the right thing or it wasn't. Painfully simple. Emphasis on the pain.

I stepped back into my shoes and walked straight out the door. The sunshine seemed violently bright. It made me squint. I flipped my cell phone open and sat down on a stone step, peering at the numbers until my eyes adjusted to the light.

Then I called 411.

While it was ringing, I was struck with a powerful and potentially liberating thought. She might not be listed. If she had an unlisted number, I was off the hook.

On came the automated voice. "What city, please?"

"San Francisco."

"What listing, please?"

"Bordatello. B-o-r-d-a-t-e-l-l-o. First name Lorraine."

A brief silence. Then a different automated voice. My esteemed cellular provider was connecting me with: I heard 415. Then the start of another number. It could have been any one of them. The guy had barely opened his computer-generated mouth.

I snapped the phone shut. Looked up to see the kid standing over me.

"Did you call her?"

"Not exactly."

"Well, what exactly?"

"I called 411."

"Did they have her number?"

"Yeah."

185

"So you're *going* to call her?"

"Not exactly." Guilty pause. "I didn't have a pen to write it down."

"Do you remember it?"

"Not exactly. I hadn't heard quite all of it when I hung up."

She sighed dramatically. More irritating role reversals. "Gimme that," she said.

Like the whipped puppy I had temporarily become, I did.

She stepped up to two middle-aged women who were standing at the cathedral entrance, talking. "Excuse me," I heard her say. "I'm sorry to bother you. But do either of you have a pen I could borrow?"

Note to self: the kid can be civilized if she knows it's in her best interests. Remind her of that when we get to Grandma's house.

I watched miserably as she made her way back to me, dialing my phone as she walked. "Bor-da-tell-o, right?"

"Right."

"You're not going to tell me what a bordello is, are you?"

"Not for several years, no."

"San Francisco," she said. But not to me. "Bordatello. Lorraine." I watched her write the number down on the inside of her left hand. She closed up my phone and handed it back to me. "What now, boss?"

"Now you go give the nice lady her pen back."

"She said I could keep it."

"Are you telling the truth?" It was a cheap plastic ball-point, so she probably was.

186

"Does she look like she's waiting to get it back?" We both turned to look, but the women had gone inside the church or otherwise disappeared. "You never trust me."

"And you're so damn trustworthy."

"Stop ducking the question. What now?"

"Now I guess I call her." Or maybe we should go get an ice cream first. Or lunch. Or a stiff drink. Or five. Or a pack of cigarettes. Or an overseas vacation.

But I knew it was better right here, right now. In the figurative shadow of Grace. If I didn't do it now, I might never. I would have to turn off my thoughts and feelings and just dial. Like I'd promised I would on the labyrinth. I didn't know anybody who'd ever lied to a labyrinth. I wasn't sure what exactly would be the penalty involved. I just knew in my gut that it didn't sound like a wise option.

I held the kid's left hand out to the proper reading distance and dialed.

James's mother answered on the fourth ring. Which was hard. You know? Because that was right around the time I was experiencing the overwhelming relief of thinking it was going to go to voice mail or a machine. That wonderful, soul-satisfying rush of comfort, like a drug. Like nicotine. But then she answered.

"Hello-o." She made it into three syllables.

I loved her immediately. She sounded like a mother. Not like *my* mother exactly, but maybe like my mother should have been. Like all mothers should be. Her voice was open. Strong. Emotional, but in a positive way. Like the tooth fairy, if the tooth fairy were real. Like Christmas, if Christmas were somebody's mother. Then I thought,

Don't love her. If you love her, you won't be able to bring yourself to tell her the truth. My heart was pounding. I'm not sure how long this thought process took.

"Hello? Is anybody there?"

"Um. Yes."

"Who is this?" But still like Christmas. Not like I should have told her already. Even though I should have told her already.

I tried to focus off the fact that the kid was staring at me. "Um. My name is Theresa. You don't know me." A pause. As if it were her turn to say something. But of course it was still my turn. It took me a moment to accept that. "I was a friend of your son. James. Your late son. I'm sorry."

For what, at this point, was unclear.

"Oh, Theresa. His next-door neighbor? Oh, how wonderful! James told me so much about you."

"He did?"

"Oh, yes. Every time he called or wrote he talked about you. He thought quite highly of you."

Silence. Dead silence on my end. I knew it was my turn, but that didn't help. He shouldn't have thought highly of me. He was wrong to have done that.

I wanted to say, I hope it's okay that I called. But nothing came out.

"It's wonderful of you to call me," she said.

A jolt of terror. She reads minds. If she knows that, she knows everything.

"It is?"

"Yes, it's wonderful. I don't know many people who knew James. And even the ones who did, they knew him as a little boy. Or a teenager. I don't know who his friends were after he left home. Except you."

I wondered if there *was* anybody except me.

"I thought maybe it would be hard for you to talk about him."

"A little," she said. "But *not* talking about him is even harder. How far away are you? You should come for a visit sometime."

Oh God. It's not my imagination. She reads minds. "I'm at Grace Cathedral."

"Oh, you're in town! I had no idea. I thought you were calling from home."

"No, I'm in San Francisco."

"Well, you should come for a visit."

"When?"

"Well, anytime, really. I'm retired. So I'm mostly home. How long are you going to be in town?"

"Not long. I need to take this friend of mine to her grandmother's in Washington State. So we'll need to get back on the road soon."

"Come today, then."

"Um." Was there still any way out? No. There really never had been. I just hadn't known it. Until now. "Okay. Yeah. That would be great. What's your address?"

I grabbed the kid's left hand again, but it was pretty full with numbers, so I wrote the address down on her arm.

"Okay, then. Thanks. Soon."

As soon as I was off the phone the kid said, "I'm glad I come in so handy. I didn't know I had a future as a notepad."

"She sounded so happy I called."

"Good."

"Not really."

She waited. We both waited. I watched people bustle up and down the street. Climb the stairs to the cathedral. Watched cars and cabs try to squeeze around double-parked vehicles. All these people had lives. I just didn't imagine any of them could be as complicated and hard as the one I was living just in that moment.

But maybe that's one of those things we think because we're only on the inside of ourselves. Not anybody else.

"Maybe I should just let her stay happy."

The kid said nothing. I said nothing.

I put my head in my hands and tried to create a dark space. A cave. Something that would cover me. Allow me to hide. If only for just a few minutes.

I'm not sure how long I sat like that. I thought it was maybe ten minutes. But when I opened my eyes, I could swear that the sun was on a noticeably different slant. And the right thing was still the right thing.

My hiding days were over.

FIVE

The Best I Can Do

I swear it must have been some kind of cosmic joke. When we found the address, it came complete with a parking space. Just sitting there. Open. Right in front of her house.

"Spooky," the kid said. She'd been a little spooked since I dragged her into a big church.

"It's unusual," I said. Thinking it was spooky, but not wanting to commit.

"It's a sign. Admit it."

"Let's not talk for a minute."

I had to take three shots at the parallel parking thing, because at home I never got to practice. When I had pretty well snugged the car in, I asked the kid to open the door and see if I was close enough to the curb.

"Yeah," she said. "We can probably hike to the curb from here."

"You're such a smart-ass."

"Thank you."

It struck me that anyone who met us would assume we were sisters. And not just because of the hair thing, either.

I turned off the engine. My hands were shaking again. I gripped the wheel tightly and we sat awhile.

"What are we doing?" she asked.

"We're getting ourselves together," I said.

"Oh."

But the more I sat, the more impossible it seemed to move. My lower body felt like hardening cement. Heavier and more inflexible with every passing second. I knew if I was going to do this, I'd better do it fast.

"Okay, I'm going in. I think you should wait here."

"Okay."

"I have no idea how long this will take."

"It's okay."

"It's just something I need to do by myself, okay?"

"It's okay. Will you just go?"

"Oh. Right. Okay."

Something in my head was causing the world to take on a dreamlike quality. I felt floaty and too acutely aware of every tiny movement. I opened the door. A car blared its horn and swerved to avoid hitting my door, and I jumped. It had never occurred to me to look before I threw my door open into traffic.

James's mother's house was dark green and narrow. That classic San Francisco narrow. Three stories, but built straight up. And the street was steep. I was standing on the side of a hill, staring at the house, and the house was straight, but I wasn't. It seemed too much like a metaphor. Or maybe I was still dreaming.

The door was white, with a brass knocker.

I'm not sure how long I stared at it before I walked back to the car. This time I checked traffic before opening my door and getting in.

"Now what are we doing? You're not chickening out, are you?"

"No. I'm not. I just need another minute."

A pause, which I expect lasted about a minute.

Then she said, "Want me to go in with you?"

That snapped me out of my dream state. Somewhat. "No. I can do this."

I threw the door open, forgetting again to watch for traffic. This time I got lucky. No cars.

I walked, rather boldly I thought, up to James's mother's front door. I raised my hand to knock. I'm not sure what happened with the follow-through on that, but next thing I remember I was turned around, facing the car. Watching the look on the kid's face. She looked scared. I saw the fear on her face and knew she must be feeling it for me. On my behalf. It brought up some feelings of my own. It reminded me to panic.

Something gave way inside my gut. I don't know how to describe it any better than that. Something in that normally solid area of my gut started to cave and slide like a rain-soaked hillside in Southern California. Houses that had stood for years began to slip, their foundations crumbling. I took two steps toward the safety of the car and then sat down. Right there in the middle of the sidewalk. I was in a full-on state of crumple.

A second or two later the kid was there, standing over me. "Now what are we doing?"

"I'm not sure. Falling apart, I think."

"Want me to knock?"

"Yeah. I guess you better. You better knock for me."

"Okay. You stay here. I'll go knock."

A few seconds later, I felt a hand on my shoulder.

I looked up into James's mother's face.

She looked a little different than I expected. She didn't exactly look like Christmas. Or if she did, she looked like a pretty shopworn and threadbare version. She looked tired. She was a little overweight, and it showed a lot around her face and chin. She had crow's-feet at the corners of her eyes and jowls that sagged. But under that was the something I'd heard on the phone. The Christmas tooth fairy. She looked like a bright shiny angel that had been baked too long, left out in the rain to rust, faded in the sun, and then developed a maze of cracks. But the cracks were a good thing, because they let the bright angel shine through.

I think I was still experiencing that dreamlike sense of everything.

"Are you okay?" she asked. Her voice was already deeply familiar to me. I knew it would haunt me, even thirty years from now, even if I never heard it again.

"Sort of. I think."

"Are you sick?"

"No. Not exactly. I just got sort of dizzy. Well, not exactly dizzy, exactly. But something."

"You look like you've been sick."

It struck me that she might be referring to my near baldness, for which she was unprepared. "If you mean the hair, I didn't have chemo. I shaved it myself. Hard to explain. It was stupid. Really stupid. I see that now."

And I really did. Sitting in the middle of the sidewalk, meeting James's mother for the first time, I could easily see how stupid that had been. I had a flash that a number of previously unseen truths could be revealed to me at any moment. And probably would be.

It was not a welcome feeling.

She reached a hand down to help me to my feet.

I sat on the couch in the front room, my hands wrapped around a cup of hot tea. I was blowing on it as if trying to warm myself. But it wasn't cold in the room. I wasn't cold. But I was shivering. Uncontrollably. My teeth were even chattering.

But I wasn't cold.

James's mother was perched on the end of the couch, watching me as though I might evaporate or explode at any moment, and I was in no position to assure her otherwise. The kid was watching silently, almost invisible in a chair in the corner. I mean, I could see her. Of course. But she was doing her best imitation of an invisible girl. I figured she'd had a lot of practice.

When I looked at the kid, I got one of those moments of sudden access to a previously unseen truth. In a couple of days, she'd have to tell her own grandmother that she'd shot the woman's other grandchild. And the phoneless grandmother might be hearing about it for the first time. I hadn't even thought of that.

She looked back at me. Met my eyes and whatever they contained. "Do you want me to wait outside?"

"No. I changed my mind. I think you should be here."

I looked back to James's mother. She seemed to have gathered that this was not a happy little visit.

She said, "You don't look the way I expected."

"What did you expect?" It was hard to talk with chattering teeth. And it was only getting worse.

"James used to talk about you all the time. He said you were very confident. And strong and capable and funny."

"That was before."

"Before what?"

"Before James . . . did what he did."

Her eyes softened even more. As if such a thing were possible. "Oh, honey. Did he mean that much to you? I'm glad. I know he was in love with you. That was so obvious."

"I came here to tell you something really hard." My teeth chattered humiliatingly as I tried to form the words.

"Yes, I sensed that."

"It was my fault."

Silence. I squeezed my eyes shut. Trying to figure out which would be worse. Looking or not looking. I stole a quick glance at James's mother. She didn't look furious. She didn't seem ready to scream at me. Instead she was smiling sadly.

"I used to feel the same way," she said. "In some ways I suppose I still do. But I'm learning to try to get over it."

"No, you don't understand. It really was my fault. I hurt him. I broke his heart."

"Well, then shame on you," she said. "Shame on you for breaking his heart. We should all be much more careful with each other's hearts. I broke a boy's heart once. In college. John." I watched the kid wince at the sound of the name. "I ran into his best friend almost twenty years later, and it turned out that in some small place in himself, John never entirely got over that. We take the treatment of someone else's heart altogether too lightly. When someone gives you his heart, it's a huge responsibility. I hope you'll do better next time."

"If there even *is* a next time. You don't seem to understand."

"Honey. Let me tell you what *you* don't understand. James had been fighting on and off with depression since he was fourteen years old. I had to hospitalize him twice for depression. He refused to take his medication after he left home. And this was his third suicide attempt. And the other two were deadly serious, believe me. Not the old 'cry for help' syndrome. He really tried. It was just by luck that he failed."

My eyes came up to hers and stayed there for the longest time. "I thought . . ."

"I know what you thought. You're a young girl, and young people think they're more powerful than they really are. You think you can make people do things. But when you get older you figure out that people only do what they had it in them to do anyway. You could have broken another boy's heart, and it would have been a terrible thing to do, but he wouldn't have killed himself. That doesn't let you off the hook for being careless with James's heart, or anybody else's for that matter. We have to take charge of what's really ours. I've spent these months blaming myself, too. If only I'd left his father sooner. His father was just awful to him. Oh, he never hit him or anything. If he had, I'd have been out the door in a second. He just was so impatient with James. He never praised him. He was so short-tempered. Nothing James did was ever good enough."

My gut was still trembling, but now I could speak without my teeth knocking together. "He was careless with James's heart."

"And I was, too, by not leaving sooner. There's plenty of blame to go around, honey, but nobody drove that motorcycle off that cliff except James. It's so sad, really. I always wanted James to find love, because I thought love was the one thing that might nail him down to this earth. But now I see that was impossible. Because he couldn't handle even the slightest disappointment. And no one will ever find love that doesn't contain the slightest disappointment. It doesn't exist, as far as I know."

SIX

My Pretending Days Are Over

"I hope you don't mind if it's just marinara sauce," she said. "I'm a vegetarian."

"I don't mind at all."

"What about your sister. Will she mind?"

"Sis?" I called into the dining room. Sis was in there setting the table. She could be polite and helpful when she got it in her head to be. I made a mental note to remind her of that when we got to Grandma's house. "You're okay with vegetarian spaghetti, right?"

"I love spaghetti. Any kind of it."

"This is nice of you," I said. I was leaning with my back against her refrigerator door. Eating from a little dish of mixed nuts and watching her peel cloves of garlic on an old-fashioned chopping block.

"Well, you have to eat. No wonder you were so shaky. Not eating all day."

"I also quit smoking about a week ago."

We both pretended that was why. At least, I think she was doing it, too.

While we pretended, I watched her press the garlic into a little dish of butter she'd softened in the microwave. She sliced a loaf of French bread into thick pieces without cutting all the way through the bottom crust. Then she slathered garlic butter in between the slabs. The leftover butter she spread on top of the loaf, which she then sprinkled with Parmesan cheese. I had personally watched her grate this cheese a few moments earlier.

As she slid the bread into the oven to bake, I was almost overcome with my own sense of awe. Nobody ever did this at my house. I thought stuff like this only happened in movies and on television. I tried to remember the last time I ate a hot meal that somebody had actually cooked at home, from scratch. But my memory fields came up disturbingly blank. If this was normal, you couldn't prove it by my background.

I said, "You know, I'm not saying you're wrong about what you said before. How young people think they're more powerful than they really are. But it was weird when you called me a young girl. I don't feel like one."

She glanced over her shoulder at me as the kid came back through for a small stack of plates. Be careful with those, I thought. They looked lovely and fragile.

"I don't imagine you do," she said. Sizing me up with her eyes. As if measuring the situation and talking about it at exactly the same time. "You sure don't talk like one.

In some ways you don't act like one, and in other ways you do. How old are you?"

"Eighteen."

"That's a young girl. I expect somewhere down the road you were pressed into service as an adult. Am I right?"

I had to think about that. I had never really looked at it that way.

"When my mom left. I guess. My father was there, but not really. You know? You could look over and see him there. On the rare occasions he was home. But even when he was there, he was never really there. Know what I mean?"

"Oh yes. I do."

"So, yeah. I guess I had to be grown-up."

"Too bad. You had a right to be a girl and have parents. Everybody needs a mother. Even grown-ups need a mother. I still need a mother, and mine's been dead for seven years."

"I'm sorry."

"If you ever need a mother so badly you can't stand it, come back and see me again. I have a big vacancy in that department."

Amazingly, that's when I started to cry for real. The kind of crying where you think you'll never stop but it's too late and you don't really care anymore anyway. Not when James washed up on the beach. Not when I told his mother it was my fault. When she offered to loan me some motherhood, I just fell apart.

She brought me a whole box of tissues.

"I'm sorry," I said. And because she was there, I took a huge, shaky breath and tried to pull it all back in again.

"Stop that," she said. "Don't do that."

So I tried even harder to stop.

"Stop trying to hold it back," she said.

Oh. She didn't mean stop crying. She meant stop stopping. "But I hate crying."

"Sure you do. Who doesn't? I hate throwing up. It's an ugly process. But if I have poison in my belly making me sick I'm not going to try to hold it in. Your body's trying to tell you something. Probably to stop pretending you don't need anything. And that you don't hurt."

If I hadn't been crying already, that would have done the job, too.

We sat at the table, in front of our vegetarian spaghetti and garlic bread. Observing a spontaneous moment of silence. I knew the kid was hungry. Because our eating habits lately had been atrocious. But she waited and didn't touch her fork. Just watched to see when someone else would.

I wondered who had taught her to be civilized.

James's mother said, "Do you say grace at your house?" Still thinking, I guess, that we came from the same house.

"Not really," I said.

"I don't believe in God," the kid said. Every time she said it, it sounded more and more like whistling in the graveyard.

"I usually like to say a little Buddhist prayer. You might like it, because it's really not so much about a traditional God idea."

"I like Buddhism," the kid said.

"You know something about Buddhism?" I said.

"Well. I think I'd like it."

"Well, then I'll say it," James's mother said. "This food is the gift of the whole Universe. Each morsel is a sacrifice of life. May I be worthy to receive it. May the energy in this food give me the strength to transform my unwholesome qualities into wholesome ones. I am grateful for this food. May I realize the Path of Awakening, for the sake of all beings." Silence. *"Namaste."*

"Amen," the little atheist said.

James's mother picked up her fork and we both followed suit.

It only took about ten bites before I felt the food changing everything inside me. The jangling feeling in my stomach and chest began to ease up. My brain began slowing down. I was weirdly exhausted from the crying, and the more I ate, the more I lost that adrenaline-rush energy and began to feel naplike. Sleepy. Grounded.

Like I wasn't dreaming.

James's mother said, "I hope you're not going to try to push on tonight. You look like you need a good sleep."

"No, I think we'll need to stop over another night." I pictured the drab little motel—or one just like it—in the empty space behind my eyes.

"Good. I've got an inflatable mattress. I'll put that in James's old room, and then you should both be pretty comfortable."

I swallowed hard and was momentarily overcome by

this entirely new thought. "I know this sounds really stupid, but it only just now occurred to me that James used to live in this house. I'm not sure why. Like I was thinking of it as a place you moved to after he left home or something."

"No, we moved here when I left his father. James lived here for five years."

We ate in silence until the kid said, "This is really good."

"It really is," I said. Trying to remember how long I'd been living on fast food, power bars, and trail mix. "Thank you. For everything."

"I'm glad you two came to visit," she said. "I think it's the things we don't talk about that make us old before our time."

We followed her up one flight of stairs, and she stopped briefly, her hand on the knob of a closed door. She turned to see that we were both right behind her.

Then she opened the door.

The walls of James's room were blue. A deep, rich blue. The bed was a small wood-framed single with a soccer-themed bedspread. One whole wall was lined with metal shelves covered with trophies. Some were cup-shaped, others shaped like a soccer player or ball, others like a hockey stick or puck. On the dresser was a photo of James, looking about my age or a little younger, in his soccer uniform. One foot on the ball.

"I'll go get the blow-up mattress," she said.

While she was gone, the kid and I both looked around. At what few books he'd abandoned, his soccer posters.

The room was missing all the miscellaneous items that clutter a room someone currently lives in. It was like a skeleton of what he had chosen to leave behind. I picked up the photo and held it in my hands. James's hair was long and shaggy in the picture. I had never seen him like that. His smile seemed wide and natural. And yet, looking at both the eyes and the smile, I could still see it. Or maybe I was reading something in. No. I wasn't. I could see it. A little cloud of darkness that the smile couldn't quite cover.

A question was forming in my head, but I didn't quite have it in words yet. I looked up to see James's mother. Holding the folded, deflated mattress. Watching me hold the photo.

"So James left home when he was eighteen, right?"

"That's right."

"So there's something I don't get." She didn't ask. Just waited. I still didn't quite have it together in my head. I looked at the picture again. "So usually when a kid dies, people keep his room just exactly the way it was. Like a shrine, you know? But usually when he just leaves home, they turn it into a sewing room or something."

I could almost hear and feel the kid standing behind me, frozen in her respect for the moment.

"I guess," James's mother said, "if I were to be perfectly honest . . . I guess part of me always knew how the story was going to end."

I was pulling off my shirt when I heard the kid pad back across the hall from the bathroom. The door opened. She popped in. I was standing there in just jeans and a bra.

"Oh. Sorry," she said. Her eyes firmly glued to the tattoo.

"It's okay. Whatever." I pressed my eyes open and shut a few times. They were sore from crying. As if someone had sandpapered the edges of my eyelids.

I pulled on my big oversize T-shirt pajamas and pulled my bra out from under it, one arm at a time. Slid my jeans out from underneath and then climbed into bed. I stared at the picture of James on the soccer field until the kid turned out the light.

"I brushed my teeth," she said.

"Good deal."

"Some day, huh?"

"Yeah. Some day."

"Are you gonna always keep the tattoo?"

"Well, tattoos are like that. They're pretty much designed for keeping."

"You can have a tattoo removed."

"I'm not going to have it removed." She didn't ask why. But I felt I needed to say why anyway. "I just figure somebody needs to remember him. I just think everybody should have at least one person—besides their mother—who always remembers them. So I guess I'll be James's one person."

"That's good."

"Think so?"

"Yeah."

Long silence. Long enough that I thought she might have gone to sleep. Except there was no snoring. "You want to talk about what happened with John?"

"No."

"You sure?"

"Yeah. I'm sure." Another long silence. I was trying to make out the shape of the photo on the dresser in the dark. "I miss John," she said. "Do you miss James?"

"Yeah. I do."

"Okay. Good night, then."

"Good night."

If she snored that night, I never heard. I must've slept through it. I think I could've slept through just about anything.

I hadn't had much experience with emotion. I had no idea how draining it could be.

SEVEN

Sudden Turns

"I think we're lost again," I said.

"No, it's this way. I know it is."

"Then why did we just pass a sign that said we're leaving Bellingham?"

"Because she's not right inside the city. That's all. She's just a little closer to Canada."

"Wait. How much closer to Canada?"

"I don't know."

"Then how do you know we didn't pass it?"

"It's this way. I know it is. I recognize this road."

"Which is exactly what you said the last three times just before we figured out we were lost." We had driven straight through the night. Now it was light, but I was dead tired and needing to take a break.

"This time I'm sure."

"Look, we might want to—"

"There it is!"

I looked but saw nothing unusual. Yet another length of tree-lined road, orange and gold leaves skittering across it in the wind. "Where?"

"That's her fish mailbox. I'd know it anywhere. Stop! You're passing it."

I hit the brake. Put the car in reverse. Not a soul on this road with us. Not ahead, not behind. Not anywhere.

We pulled level with the fish mailbox. It didn't just have fish painted on it, as I had been imagining. It was actually shaped like a fish. It had one red wooden fin that could be raised as a mail flag. Under the fin it said, in clean white fluorescent stick-on letters, WEISS.

"I guess we're here," I said.

I turned into the hard-packed dirt driveway and was surprised to drive for nearly half a mile without seeing a house.

"She likes to live far away from people," the kid said.

"I gathered that." I was also gathering that it could work against us. But of course I didn't say so.

We eased around a final bend and there it all was. A house. And a grandmother. The house was wood, freshly painted. Light blue, with white trim and white shutters. The grandmother was sweeping off the front porch. She wore an old-fashioned housedress and sneakers. And an apron. A cigarette dangled from her lips as she swept.

Her eyes came up to meet us, and my heart fell. She glared. Suspicious. Hostile. I was reminded of the old movies where the farmer runs to fetch his shotgun the minute some unwelcome visitor drives up.

As we stepped out of the car, she came toward us, down the first two porch steps, shading her eyes from the sun. We stood at the bottom of the steps, looking up at her. No one said anything for a long time. Well, half a minute. But it felt long.

The grandmother spoke first. "You're Cathy." She had a husky voice. Scratchy, like car tires crunching over gravel.

"Yes, ma'am," the kid said.

"You come to tell me what happened with John. But I know already. I know all about that. Your mom, she wrote me a letter. Tried to make it sound like it was all your fault. Bull, I say. You don't give a kid a gun and tell her, Watch the place. You do, you're to blame whatever happens then on. That mother of yours never was any good."

"Yes, ma'am."

"Nice of you to come tell me, anyway. You come a long way?"

"We came from California," I said.

"Had breakfast?"

"No, ma'am," I said. It was contagious. Also, I found her a little intimidating.

"Least I can do is feed you a good breakfast before you head back."

She turned and walked up the porch steps again, motioning us to follow.

I opened my mouth to speak, but the kid kicked my foot. "What?" I whispered.

"Don't."

"We have to ask her. We came all this way."

"She'll say no."

"We still have to try."

We followed her into the kitchen, through a living room choked with overstuffed furniture and hand-knit afghans and a spinning wheel and a sewing machine and an old-fashioned jukebox and an ancient upright piano and dozens of other things I had no time to inventory with my eyes.

"I'll put on coffee," she said, seating us at her old Formica kitchen table. "You drink coffee?"

"Yes, ma'am," the kid and I said in exact unison.

"I was talking to *her*. You're too young," she said, pointing at the kid with the fingers that still held the cigarette. The ash was nearly an inch long and looked ready to fall off at any time.

"Mrs. Weiss," I said. At the corner of my eye I saw the kid tighten up all over. "We didn't just come here to tell you about John. There's more to the visit than that."

She rattled through the contents of a kitchen cupboard until she found coffee filters. "State it, then," she said without turning to look at me.

"Cathy's mother threw her out."

"That woman never was any good."

"She's got no place to go."

She turned around then. Really focused on me for the first time. I watched it dawn on her. What was happening. Why we were really here. She looked at me through narrow eyes, then looked at the kid. Then back at me.

"You're the only blood family she's got," I said.

"Well, that's true enough. But I don't know. I'm not as

young as I used to be. And coming from that mother of hers . . ."

"She can be a good kid," I said. The kid's eyes came up to me, but I couldn't really take the time to look back. "I know her pretty well now. She can be a nice kid. It's almost like nobody ever gave her a reason to be."

"So what you're saying is, she *can* be good . . . but mostly she's not."

I realized we were talking about her as if she weren't here, but I couldn't think what to do about that. I glanced over at her. She was staring at the tabletop. Running the tip of her finger along the patterns.

"What I'm saying is . . . she doesn't need much. She's not a baby. She's been raising herself for a long time now. She needs a roof over her head and food and somebody to sign her up for school now that it's fall. She can be a help to you, too. And I think she will. I really think she'll be a good girl if you take her in."

"And what makes you so sure she'll turn over a new leaf all of a sudden?"

"That's easy. You're her last hope. No Plan B. The best motivator there is."

Grandma disappeared briefly into a little pantry area by the back door. Came back holding a small wire basket with a handle. She handed this to the kid. "Cathy, you run out back to the henhouse and gather up half a dozen eggs."

"Yes, ma'am."

When she was well down the back steps and gone, the grandmother turned to face me, hands on hips. But by then her cigarette was burned down to the filter, so she ran it under water at the kitchen sink and threw it into a lined plastic trash bin.

I was waiting for her to say no.

"Lord," she said. "Life turns on a dime, don't you think? Woke up this morning thinking I'd spend the day picking apples and putting apple butter up in Ball jars. You wake up and you think you know just how your life's gonna go. Nice and simple. Turns out the world got a different idea for you. Like I always say, man plans, God laughs."

"Does this mean you'll take her?"

"Blood family, I guess I at least gotta try. But she has to be good."

"I will be," the kid said.

We both looked up to see Cathy standing in the back doorway. Panting. Holding a basket half full of eggs.

"That was quick," Grandma said.

"I'll be good. I can help out around here. I will. Gimme a chance."

"Okay, a chance. Everybody ought to get a chance. But I got rules here."

"That's okay. Rules are okay."

Grandma lifted the basket of eggs out of her hands. "Where's your stuff, girl? You got a suitcase in her car?"

The kid didn't answer, so I answered for her. "Her mother threw her out with just the clothes on her back."

"That woman never was any good."

"But if you want," I said, "when I get back home . . . I'll be getting a job, and I could send some money along. So she can get some clothes and stuff."

"No thanks. Nice offer, but we'll make do. I can sew. And I'll take her down to the church thrift store. Little goes a long way there."

The kid sat back down at the table with me. We watched her grandmother breaking eggs into a hot skillet. She hadn't asked how we wanted them. I guess it was more a question of how she wanted to cook them.

The kid spoke up suddenly, surprising both of us. And maybe even herself. "Do I have to go to church?"

A long silence.

"Nope. I don't suppose. I been going by myself for a long time. Guess I can go by myself just as well now."

"Good. Because I'm a Buddhist."

"A Buddhist! Oh Lord. I forgot. You're from California. Well, I guess as long as you believe in *something* I don't guess I got the right to say what. Not that you could prove it by looking around at the world, but I guess people can get along in spite of their religious differences. You want apple butter on your toast?"

"Yes, ma'am," we both said, once again in perfect unison.

"She blames herself for what happened," I told Mrs. Weiss.

We were out on the front porch. She was sitting on the porch swing, rocking and knitting. I was perched on the railing, the hot sun on my back.

Cathy was out back proving her worth by picking the apples that her grandmother would put up in Ball jars later in the day.

"We're always hardest on ourselves," she said.

"Right now I can't even get her to talk about it."

"I'll try and make sure she doesn't punish herself."

"You can't stop her," I said. "I'm not even sure you should try. I know it sounds weird. But I sort of have this theory." But I'd never said it out loud before. In fact, I'd never even put it together in this order in my head. I would have to organize these thoughts as I went along. "I wasn't there when the police questioned her. But she's here. So they must've ruled it accidental."

"They did. As well they should have, don't you think?"

"Well, yeah. Of course. From their point of view, of course it was an accident. But from hers, it would almost have been better if they'd decided to punish her. Because then she wouldn't have to punish herself. And like you said, we're always hardest on ourselves. I mean, if they'd ruled that there was some kind of negligence or something. Manslaughter. They'd have locked her up for a few years. But then when she got out, she could say, Hey, I paid my debt to society. I'm off the hook. It's over. But when we punish ourselves, there's nobody to let us out and tell us we're free now. It's hard to know when to stop. So instead of telling her not to blame herself . . . maybe you could just help her see when it's time to stop."

She looked up from her knitting for the first time. Leveled me with a hard look. "Sounds like you know a thing or two about it."

"I do. Actually."

"I'm sorry you have to be such an expert on the subject."

"Thanks," I said. "Me too." I watched her knit a few rows. It was addictive, even to watch. Of course, I was tired. Then I said, "I think you two'll get along okay."

"Yeah. And no. We're both stubborn. We'll butt heads. It'll be hard. Lord. My life had just finally got simple. Still and all, I look back on the times my life was simple and the times it was hard. And somehow it's always the hard ones I wouldn't trade."

The kid walked me out to the car.

"Maybe I could call you," she said.

"You don't have a phone."

"Oh. Right. Maybe I could write to you. Will you write back?"

"Yes. I will."

"Promise?"

"Yes," I said. "I promise I won't be careless with your heart."

An awkward silence. We were clearly skirting the line of mushiness, and neither one of us was the mushy type. To put it mildly.

"Thanks," she said.

I poked her forehead with my index finger. It was as close to a gesture of affection as we were about to get. "I owed you one after San Francisco."

"Very true."

"Promise me you won't steal cigarettes from that woman."

216

"I won't. I quit."

"For real?"

"If you quit, I quit. You better stop and sleep."

"I will."

And I did.

I took Highway 1 down the coast, so I could stop at the Castle and tell Art and Leander and Todd I was alive and doing okay. Assuming they even cared. But I was willing to take the risk.

Of course, that took me right by "The Place." The cross and wreath were still intact. I pulled over and parked. Looked off to the edge of the bluff. I hadn't been out there. You know. Since.

I walked out, right to the edge. Looked down and got that strange dizzy sensation of height. Dropped to my knees without realizing I was doing it. Said this:

"I am so, so sorry I was careless with your heart. Can you ever forgive me?"

The answer was right there in front of my face. Immediately. The cool ocean wind blew the answer right into my eyes and ears: I would never know. Fairly or unfairly, I would never get to find out whether James could eventually have found it in his heart to forgive me. That's just the way it was, and I had no choice but to accept it.

So then, the only important question left was whether I could ever forgive myself.

It was a relief, really. A comfort. The only critical question still on the table was totally within my power to answer. All by myself.

Also by Catherine Ryan Hyde:

Becoming Chloe
★ "Deeply affecting. . . . This is eloquent storytelling about how two troubled teens find redemption—through each other."
—*Publishers Weekly,* Starred

★ "Tender, amazingly hopeful . . . vibrant and heartbreaking."
—*Kirkus Reviews,* Starred

The Year of My Miraculous Reappearance
"Reminiscent of the evocative style of S. E. Hinton. . . . Very close to perfect." —*The Philadelphia Inquirer*

"Hyde offers a gritty subject without making the story gritty. Always heartfelt, always suspenseful. . . . Few such regeneration books have the capacity to actually reach young people trapped in addiction; this one might." —*Kirkus Reviews*